SHADOWS OF MEN

JIM TULLY

SHADOWS OF MEN

ILLUSTRATED
BY
WILLIAM
GROPPER

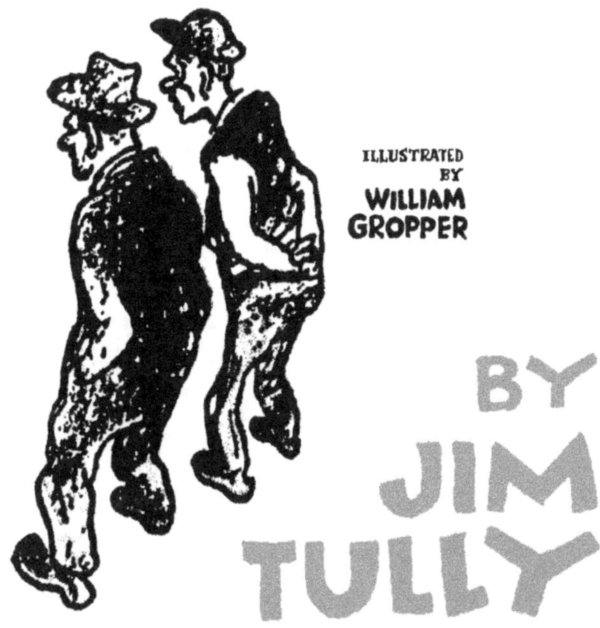

BY
JIM
TULLY

Introduction by Paul J. Bauer & Mark Dawidziak

Commonwealth Book Company
St. Martin, Ohio

ISBN: 978-1-948986-68-7

TO

ALBERT LEWIN

AND

PAUL BERN

FOR UNDERSTANDING

NONE OF THE CHARACTERS
IN THIS BOOK ARE COMPLETELY IMAGINARY

"Distrust all in whom the impulse to punish is powerful.

"They are people of bad race and lineage; out of their countenances peer the hangman and the sleuth-hound.

"Distrust all those who talk much of their justice! Verily, in their souls not only honey is lacking.

"And when they call themselves 'the good and just,' forget not, that for them to be Pharisees, nothing is lacking—but power!"

NIETZSCHE

CONTENTS

INTRODUCTION

Paul J. Bauer and Mark Dawidziak

JIM TULLY (June 3, 1886 – June 22, 1947) was an American writer who won critical acclaim and commercial success in the 1920s and '30s. His rags-to-riches career may qualify him as the greatest long shot in American literature. Born near St. Marys, Ohio, to an Irish immigrant ditch-digger and his wife, Tully enjoyed a relatively happy but impoverished childhood until the death of his mother in 1892. Unable to care for him, his father sent him to an orphanage in Cincinnati. The nuns taught him to read and write but life at the orphanage left him overwhelmed with sadness and an abiding sense that he was truly alone in the world. After six years, although still a child, he became too old for the orphanage and was dismissed. He left with what little formal education he would receive. He also left with a sense of alienation that would haunt him for the rest of his life. He hopped a train and what further education he acquired came in the hobo camps, boxcars, railroad yards, and public libraries scattered across the country. Finally, after six years and weary of the road, he arrived in Kent, Ohio, where he worked as a chainmaker, professional boxer, and tree surgeon. He also began to write, mostly poetry, which was published in the area newspapers.

Tully moved to Hollywood in 1912, where he began writing in earnest. His literary career took two distinct paths. He became one of the first reporters to cover Hollywood. As a free-lancer, he was not constrained by the studios and wrote about Hollywood celebrities (including Charlie Chaplin, for whom he had worked) in ways that they did not always find agreeable. For these pieces, rather tame by current standards, he became known as the most-feared man in Hollywood — a title he relished. Less lucrative, but closer to his heart, were the dark novels he wrote about his life on the road and the American underclass. He also wrote an affectionate memoir of his childhood with his extended Irish family, as well as novels about prostitution, boxing, Hollywood, and a travel book. While some of the more graphic books ran afoul of the censors, they were also embraced by critics, including H. L. Mencken, George Jean Nathan, and Rupert Hughes. Tully, Hughes wrote, "has fathered the school of hard-boiled writing so zealously cultivated by Ernest Hemingway and lesser luminaries."

By the end of the twenties, Tully could look back on a career that included six books, one of them, *Beggars of Life*, made into both a Broadway play with a young James Cagney and a film with Louise Brooks, as well as dozens of articles about Hollywood, his life on the road, or whatever might strike his fancy and pay a few bills. He had come a long way since his first book, the semi-autobiographical novel *Emmett*

INTRODUCTION

Lawler, in 1922 and the onetime road kid put his net worth in 1927 at a staggering $100,000. As a successful writer, he would have been forgiven for heading to the middle of the road for his next book. Instead, he wrote *Shadows of Men*.

The idea of men in jail had interested Tully for years, going back to his youthful reading of Dostoyevsky's *The House of the Dead* and his own time in jail and on a work crew. It was to this subject that he turned with *Shadows of Men*. He had already written about drifters and the underworld in *Beggars of Life* and *Circus Parade*, but those episodes were, respectively, part of his larger story of life as a road kid and working for a small-time circus. *Shadows of Men* would be different. Its first eighteen chapters focused exclusively on the brutal aspects of his road years. These chapters are set in hobo camps, boxcars, railroad yards, jails, and cotton fields. As Tully wrote in the foreword to a later book, *Blood on the Moon*, *Shadows of Men*, "contains the tribulations, vagaries and hallucinations of men in jail."

Tully's earlier books placed him in some semblance of a family. Whether it was his childhood family in *Shanty Irish* or the collection of freaks and outcasts in *Circus Parade*, Tully belonged to a group that accepted him. Alienation runs through every page of *Shadows of Men*. Nowhere is this more evident than in the opening chapter, "Sapping Day." Following the murder of a railroad detective in a western state, Tully and other vagrants were rounded up by vigilantes, stripped to the waist, and forced to run the gauntlet. "On both sides of us were the leering tobacco-stained faces of rustics, old, middle-aged, and young. The lashing of long whips could be heard on naked skin. The hoboes grunted and staggered on. We, the despised and rejected, ran as if it were part of the day's work." Tully's journey from the bosom of his childhood family in *Shanty Irish* to alienation and being the "other" in *Shadows of Men* was complete.

Jim and a friend escape the mob of vigilantes but are arrested in a hobo jungle for vagrancy and Jim's concealed knife. They are sentenced to 120 days. Over the next sixteen chapters Tully describes life in jail, often letting the other prisoners, an assortment of hoboes, forgers, hustlers, grifters, con men, yeggs, pyromaniacs, murderers, and drug addicts, tell their stories.

These include Brother Jonathon, a snake oil hustler, Nitro Dugan, "a past master at boiling dynamite in water" to yield nitroglycerin for blowing open safes, Dippy, a pyromaniac, and Hypo Sleigh, a cocaine and morphine addict. *Shadows of Men* is *The Canterbury Tales* in black.

Their stories are dark, gritty, and decidedly lacking in the romance of the road or class struggle. In Tully's view there is often little moral distinction between the "knights of the road" and those charged with protecting society from their predations. The chapter titled "Jungle Justice," previously published in the *American Mercury*, is illustrative.

A vagabond named One-Lung Riley came off the road and, using his knowledge of hoboes and their ways, became a notorious railroad detective. Seeking vengeance on the traitor Riley, a group of hoboes dragged him into a remote hobo jungle along the Mississippi River where he was charged with shooting hoboes in the back. A kangaroo court found him guilty and Riley was shot to death, his body consigned to the dark currents of the Mississippi. The hoboes dispersed along the paths and "In a short time the jungle was silent."

The power of the story derives not so much from the characters as from the place--dark, isolated, foreboding, dangerous, evil. In Tully's hands the hobo jungle was the stuff of nightmares.

The setting made such a strong impression after it first appeared in the *American Mercury* that when the Associated Press reported in 1929 on the destruction of the hobo jungle known as The Willows, it noted the camp was "the scene of Jim Tully's famous story, 'Jungle Justice,'..."

About midway through *Shadows of Men*, Tully briefly pauses from the narratives of his fellow prisoners to describe prison life. It is a grim and crowded world of crabs, human odor and filth (baths were available only weekly), solitary confinement, cigarettes, furtive conversations, glimpses of female prisoners, misery, and hopelessness. Tully summarized his time in jail: "We stood in a half circle, watching the door. It had become an obsession with me. For nearly four months I had watched men pass through it, with hands locked and heads bowed, to the most dismal of destinies."

While Tully's description of life on the road in *Beggars of Life* and other works anticipated Jack Kerouac's famous *On the Road* by nearly three decades, in *Shadows of Men* Tully tried his hand at subject matter later made famous by Kerouac's fellow beat writer, William Burroughs.

INTRODUCTION

In a chapter titled "Bull Horrors," which first appeared in the October 1927 *American Mercury*, Tully explored the world of the junkie. One night near Fort Worth, Jim and an older hobo, out after twenty years in prison, caught a boxcar out of town.

As the train rattled through the Texas night, Jim watched his companion fitfully smoke a cigarette. The older man fidgeted, removed his coat, and began to shake. Jim noticed his bruised and needle-scarred arms. "He fumbled in his coat pocket and took from it the small tin lid of a typewriter ribbon box. He filled it with a powder which looked yellow in the moonlight." He added water to the cocaine, struck a match, and warmed the mixture. Jim watched him draw it into a syringe made from a glass dropper and Jim tied off his arm. "He shot the dreams into his arm, and I released the rope."

Nightmares are loosed and the man's ravings swirl through the dark boxcar. He recalled a murder committed while high on heroin. "An' kid, the night o' the big trouble you should 'a' seen me. I plugged her perty, I did. I says, 'Listen, listen little girl, I'm goin' to let your soul out,' an' I spit the bullets through her double-crossin' heart…" In a low, throaty voice he continued. "And when she lay there all dead—a splotch of blood on her white waist—I fell down over her an' moaned: 'Oh, kid, oh, kid, for God's sake! I didn't mean to do it."

"Remembered pain stared from his eyes" and his ravings transformed the gloomy boxcar into a cauldron of anger, self-loathing, and remorse. As the train slowed at a crossing, Jim saw his chance and jumped off. He watched the ghostly train disappear into the night.

In the final two chapters of *Shadows of Men*, Tully returned to more familiar ground. Indeed, in a 1925 letter to H.L. Mencken, Tully claimed that the story he was writing for the *American Mercury*, and which would eventually find its way into *Shadows of Men*, "Bright Eyes," would be "devoid of all magazine tricks." He further pledged that "I'll not have to invent a single line--as life wrote the tale first." The story would be about a road kid that Tully had met in 1903.

Jim met Blink Thomas, then nicknamed Bright Eyes, at the Newsboy's Home in Chicago. Bright Eyes had worked at a print shop until ink splashed in his eye. When the eye became infected and had to be removed, leaving "an empty red socket" covered by a patch, Bright Eyes became Blink.

Years later, Jim found Blink in southern California. The one-eyed road kid was facing six months in jail unless he could find work. Despite his fear of going blind, he got a job at a Los Angeles newspaper as a printer's devil. His remaining eye, "long weakened," began to trouble him. His friends persuaded him to go to the county hospital. "When the doctors had finished there were two empty red sockets in his head." Jim recalled one hospital visit. "He would lie on the bed, his raven-black hair rolling back from his forehead, and the tears welling out of the red holes in his head like water from a spring."

When Jim visited him at the Institution for the Blind, he found his friend deeply depressed and preferring death to the years that would await him in the Institution. Jim wrote the publisher of the Los Angeles newspaper where Blink had worked seeking a downtown street corner where Blink could sell papers. His letters were never answered. Jim persisted and went to the publisher's office to make his case. The publisher, a once physically imposing man slowed by age, referred to in *Shadows of Men* as "General," blustered about unions. Jim patiently waited for an opening to make his pitch for Blink. The General was unmoved.

In an attempt to buy time, Jim visited Blink and lied that the General was considering the matter. Three months passed and Jim and his friends collected almost seventy dollars for Blink which they took to him for Christmas. They assured him that he'd get his street corner yet and changed the subject. After his visitors left, tired of waiting and tired of life, Blink escaped from the hospital on the outskirts of town and somehow traveled the four miles into the city. There he found his way to a pawnshop, bought a gun, and checked into a cheap hotel. The next morning, Blink found his way into the General's paper when the *Times* ran a brief story about the suicide of a printer named Frank Thomas.

The story had one problem. It was true — or at least close enough to the truth to make Tully's publisher, Doubleday, Doran, nervous. After reading the chapter in manuscript, Tully's editor warned him in July of 1929 that his description of General Otis, which was clearly based on the staunchly anti-union publisher of the *Los Angeles Times*, Harrison Gray Otis, would almost certainly invite a libel suit. Others who had read the piece in the *American Mercury*, also protested Tully's treatment of Otis. The chance to poke a windy and powerful man in the eye proved irresistible to Tully. The chapter stood.

The final chapter of *Shadows of Men* is unique among Tully's books, his travel book *Beggars Abroad* excepted, as it is reportage of an event Tully witnessed as an adult and long after he had come off the road. That chapter, "A California Holiday", first appeared in Mencken's *American Mercury* and describes the final minutes of a man condemned to hanging. Tully traveled to San Quentin in 1927 to observe the execution of Earl Clark. Clark had murdered a sailor who had been pursuing Clark's girlfriend, been arrested, and escaped the Los Angeles County jail. Clark settled in a small town in South Dakota and started a new life where he married and worked as a painter. His undoing was the stuff of film noir: a young man who had taken a mail-order detective course tracked down Clark and turned him in. In "A California Holiday" Tully describes Clark's execution without tears or pity.

The piece ranks with Tully's most powerful work owing to Tully's restraint in describing the growing horror as the hour of death approaches. Tully and the other men share an awful knowledge: they know the precise time and place of a man's imminent and intentional death--a knowledge that is only slightly less ghastly for the witnesses than for the condemned. It is not a static horror. As Tully notes the passing minutes, time become a palpable presence filling the chapter with tension and unspeakable dread. The men mark time discussing the condemned man's case, gazing out the window at the sun-washed bay, or nervously laughing at gallows humor. Tully studies the room, the guards, and finally the condemned man.

At the appointed hour, the prisoner was carried to the platform, a hood placed on his head, and the rope put around his neck. "The warden's hand raised. The trap sprang with an awful noise. The man's body dropped ten feet. It did not move." Tully describes but does not react to the scene. Grown men faint, others weep.

Upon the initial publication of "A California Holiday" in the *American Mercury*, letters of praise came from figures as disparate as Ruby Darrow, wife of Clarence, and Walter Winchell. Columnist Frank Scully, wrote that Tully "stood by the scaffold and watched the lad's neck pop, then sat down without a quaver of emotion or a break in a line and wrote his most hard-boiled report. Without even one aside, "A California Holiday" remains the most terrible indictment against capital punishment as yet written in America." The piece has drifted in and out of print ever since.

Reviews of *Shadows of Men* were generally good. Bruce Catton, the revered Civil War historian, declared: "Jim Tully is a strange and compelling writer. His work may delight you or it may shock and disgust you; but it will never, never bore you... There is more red blood in him than in a dozen run-of-mine novels." Tully's talent for hard-boiled realism was echoed by the *New Yorker*: "Mr. Tully is a born story-teller. He writes because he is naturally articulate and dramatic, and for the decidedly Irish pleasure of amusing, shocking, and stimulating you... He has none of the set sensationalism of your journalist making copy of desperate characters. He is not astonished or horrified that a man happens to be a murderer or a thief..." Writing for the *New York Herald Tribune*, Donald Henderson Clarke raved: "...when he is telling stories of the tough gents he knows so well he smokes along at a dizzying and sometimes a terrifying pace... He never avoids using the right word when the right word might prove offensive. He couldn't paint these characters in pastel shades..." *Time* noted that "Jim Tully does not like to be called hard-boiled himself, but the people he writes about are not ladies' men. He continues to write about the hobos he knew when he was one of them because he thinks it is good for men to know all their brothers and because not one writer in a hundred knows the idiom that he does." The *Cleveland Plain Dealer* proclaimed simply: "He has arrived."

The *New Republic*, on the other hand, unfavorably compared Tully to the more "progressive" Michael Gold, noting that, for Tully, "… the simple lives of yeggs and hoboes merely garnish his philosophy of weary misanthropy." By comparison "… the workers of Michael Gold are lighted by a passionate pity." Uplifting literature was not Tully's style.

While Doubleday professed to be disappointed in sales of *Shadows of Men*, Tully could take cold comfort that the book, like *Beggars of Life* before it, proved to be a best-seller in Russia—where royalties could not be taken out of the country. Tully was perhaps his own toughest critic and years later told the legendary editor Maxwell Perkins that *Shadows of Men* was his best book.

Critic Gerald Green seemed to agree:

Even a Neanderthaler like Jim Tully can induce a rare and believable terror, open our eyes to a kind of world that surely exists--one that we might never know about if it were not for Tully. Go back and read "Jungle Justice" in the collection *Shadows of Men*. In Tully's gnarled prose, we learn about the murder of a railroad detective named One-Lung Riley, scourge of the bindle stiffs, by a mob led by a certain Nitro Dugan. By the time Riley has been humiliated, shot, stripped, mutilated, and bound to a log for "the carp," we are sweating. Genet's pederasts, Burroughs' junkies, and all the minor scarecrows—Selby, Rechy, Schneck, LeRoi Jones – are all schoolboys alongside old Tully. And at least he has the virtue of absolute honesty, of innocence. He is not at all concerned with promoting himself; he wants to tell you a story. He is concerned with other people.

Before Dashiell Hammett, whose characters also walked mean streets and dark alleys, or Ernest Hemingway, who also wrote in short, clipped sentences, it was Jim Tully who was credited by his contemporaries with being the father of hard-boiled fiction. *Shadows of Men*, unsparing in its depiction of bleak people and places at cruel edges of the American landscape, was the book that cemented that reputation.

CHAPTER I

SAPPING DAY

WE HAD DRIFTED AS CASUAL AS THE DAWN INTO A scrawny town in a Western state. It was fringed with mountains, the tops of which were covered with snow and outlined in grandeur against the sky.

Blink Thomas was with me. He had once been known as Bright Eyes. He had been blinded in one eye. His name had then been changed to Blink.

So long had we been out of touch with civilization that we knew not the day of the week or the month. And neither did we care.

The town had for years been the headquarters of a famous railroad detective. His name was a hissing among yeggs and hoboes.

Different members of the fraternity had threatened his life many times. We arrived there three days after it had been taken at last. At an age when most boys are in school, the story of the man's death made a strong impression on us.

For over twenty years he had given no quarter to roving members of the underworld.

Months before, while on another coast-to-coast trip, I was seated at the horseshoe lunch counter of the railroad restaurant in his headquarters town. A hobo, full of liquor and loquacity, was seated near me. He was performing the kind act of buying me food.

A man with a huge sombrero, a Masonic watch charm, a diamond ring on his little finger, and a frown on his dark face seated himself next to my benefactor. My heart pumped fast. I knew from many descriptions that it was Arizona Slim, the hated detective.

But my friend, being in that happy state which admitted even detectives into his company, expanded toward him.

"Join us in some grub, 'bo. Take some Java, too; it's colder'n the North Pole outside. You may as well eat on me."

I nudged my companion.

"I'll buy my own grub," came the rasping answer. "Do you know who you're talkin' to?"

"No," replied the friend of humanity, "and I don't give a damn. I'm Syracuse Jake."

"Git up and walk," was the sudden command.

"Let them eat, Slim. They're not hurtin' anything, God knows."

I glanced at the detective, at the food, and at the woman.

As if to even the score, she was known in whatever parts of the world American hoboes traveled as a square shooter. She never refused them food and often gave them money. Many of them repaid her from far places.

Arizona Slim motioned to the door and pulled a revolver from his pocket.

He looked sternly at the woman.

"I'm a-runnin' this show. They can't hang around here for the Limited. Let 'em work and pay their way."

"But let 'em eat, anyhow"—from the woman.

"The less they eat the sooner they'll work."

"Well, you can't keep 'em from takin' food with 'em." Turning to us—"Here boys, I'll wrap you up some doughnuts."

"No, you don't," jerked Arizona Slim. "Let's walk!" He touched our sides with the revolver.

A gust of wind blew snow in our faces as the door opened.

"Well, Slim, your day'll come." The woman's voice followed us.

The Limited was due in less than an hour.

For some distance we walked ahead of the detective.

"Keep on a walkin'. Don't stop, and don't turn around, for if you do I'll put a bullet in your domes."

We walked onward through the whirling snow. My loquacious friend expostulated on the ingratitude of mankind.

"I wanted to feed him, an' look what he done."

I stopped him with, "Let's forget that; we want the blind baggage of the Limited."

My friend immediately reached a decision. He pulled a dented Ingersoll watch from his pocket.

"He'll beat it back in the warm, that guy will. Dicks hate the cold like they hate us."

We walked swiftly to an open space along the track.

"The Limited'll come in a little while now." He began to gather wood with, "Help me, kid."

In a short time we had a fire burning.

"Slim'll come out to see what's the matter, an' we'll sneak back by a roundabout way an' grab the Limited."

When the Limited left the station we were aboard. As it dashed by the fire we saw Arizona Slim gazing earnestly about.

His death was attributed to many men.

Years before a yegg had shot at him from ambush and missed.

The quick-witted detective fell to the earth and lay still. When the yegg walked toward his prostrate body the detective shot him dead. The exploit covered Arizona Slim with glory.

Once again, under a blistering sun, he heard a shot and fell to the ground. He lay for two hours, silent as chaos.

No one approached him.

At last he rose.

Two bullets ripped his life away.

Knowing that innocent vagrants were often punished for crimes they did not commit, we left the town immediately and walked nearly forty miles to a water tank at which it was said that now and then a freight train stopped.

And there we lingered two days and two nights, worn out but unable to rest, with swollen feet and sand-whipped eyes, with cracked lips and dried throats, and aching bodies upon which the rags hung loosely.

The detective's death had incensed the citizens along a thousand miles of railroad.

In the country of the enemy, and no other railroad within several hundred miles, with sand and sage desolation all about us, young in years but old in the ways of the road, we kept to the steel right of way.

We learned in the next few days that every Mexican laborer would share the last bite of his tortilla with a road kid.

We had but a slim Spanish vocabulary, but we were long schooled in the gestures of pain, so we made ourselves understood.

We came to the box-car home of a Mexican section foreman. Two box cars had been placed in the form of a T. A whitewashed paling fence not two feet high ran around them. Red and pink geraniums rioted in the center of a yellow grass-covered yard.

Just married, the man's eldest daughter had gone to live in Amarillo. The father was overjoyed. She had married beyond her station—a railroad engineer.

Another daughter, our own age, remained at home. Father and child helped us to the remnants of the wedding feast.

There was a vast quantity of tequila, a highly potent Mexican liquor, distilled from cactus.

We remained at the house until late that evening.

A curved part of the moon pushed the sun down the sky. The west was a vivid red splotch of color.

A cadaverous wanderer strolled into the yard.

He was tall and gaunt. His cheeks were hollow. His eyes opened and shut as rapidly as the ticking of a watch.

Angelina, the girl, arose as he asked hoarsely: "How's the chances for some grub, folks? I hain't eat since mornin'. I'm willin' to pay."

The Mexican, without a word, stood up and motioned him into the house. The large table with its red oilcloth still contained enough for several men.

Once he was seated the stranger's long arms reached for food in all directions. The Mexican handed him a large drink of tequila. He swallowed the powerful liquid as though it were water. His glass was filled again.

We sat about the table as he ate. No one spoke. His appetite half satisfied, he finally looked at Blink and me.

"Which way, 'boes?"

"West," I answered.

"There's a freight outta here at midnight—easy ridin', they say. I'm layin' for that." He extended his glass.

"So are we," said Blink.

There was upon him a pallor of prison that the elements had not yet obliterated.

He caught my gaze.

"What you lookin' at, kid?"

"Nothing," I evaded.

The liquor made his eyes shine. A fit of coughing seized him. It became so violent that the kindly Mexican and his daughter looked at each other in alarm.

I rose with Blink.

"We'd better be leavin', 'bo," I said, motioning to our benefactor. "He's got to go to work in the morning."

The vagabond tried to stand erect. The fury of the liquor roared in his head. Clutching the edge of the table, he finally succeeded.

We thanked the Mexicans and walked slowly down the track with our new comrade.

He gasped several times and held his right hand to his chest. He walked with bent legs. The upper part of his torso was thrown forward. His feet scraped the ground. His eyes blinked constantly. His face was twisted with agony, as though he walked barefooted on hot steel.

Ghostlike and ghastly, he was the color of a man upon whom was the dust of the grave.

He suddenly grabbed at his temples and exclaimed, "Holy God, my head!"

He began to sink. We helped him along the uneven roadbed.

"It'll soon be my turn, kid," he groaned between gasps. "Half a lung left." He threw his head back. His blinking eyes looked at the star-dotted sky. "The other cons, they said, 'You may's well git him—you'll croak before they git you anyhow.'" He breathed heavily, his hands upon our shoulders.

"He got me sent up for five years—breakin' an'

enterin'. He said it was me, an' the judge took his word—an' I never did it—never had the nerve to steal—always a workin' stiff. But I said, 'Slim, if I ever git out, it's you or me.' I'd 'a' been waitin' there yet till he got up."

We listened without surprise or comment.

Our creed, early inculcated, was to tell on no man.

We helped him into an empty box car of the midnight freight.

Exhausted, he stretched his emaciated body on the splintery floor. He was soon asleep.

Early the next morning the train was surrounded and searched. We were arrested by a group of citizens and placed in the calaboose.

The sun was not visible. Rain threatened.

A dozen vagabonds were already in the jail.

"I'll bet they're goin' to sap on us, 'cause somebody plugged Arizoner Slim," one vagrant said upon our entrance.

Hundreds of men paraded about the small town. They had come from miles around.

We soon learned that we were to be made the victims of a rustic celebration known in the district as Sapping Day.

Stripped to the waist, we were released from jail that afternoon and made to run the gantlet.

We had been given no food.

"A lean horse runs fast," said a middle-aged rustic.

We were marched to the end of a lane. Our cadaverous friend coughed often as we marched.

Lined up on each side of the lane, hundreds of men awaited us. They were well supplied with clubs, stones, and long rattan whips.

At a signal we started to run.

On both sides of us were the leering and tobacco-stained faces of rustics, old, middle aged, and young. The lashing of long whips could be heard on naked skin. The hoboes grunted and staggered on. We, the despised and rejected, ran as if it were part of the day's work.

We had not gone far when two old vagabonds fell exhausted to the ground.

A group of rustics gathered about them.

Mud was thrown in their aged faces. They tried to ward off the brutality by holding their arms over their eyes. They were kicked in the sides. Hard hands slapped viciously against their hollow cheeks.

"We'll teach you, damn you, to stay away from honest men," a rustic in a rubber collar shouted. As if to better shield themselves from the fury, the two old codgers turned on their stomachs and buried their faces in the mud.

A farmer spat tobacco juice in their ears.

They took it in silence.

A vagrant made an attempt to carry one of them

with him. He was slammed across the arms with clubs until forced to drop his burden.

Clubs and stones crashed against our feet. Ahead was freedom. How far we knew not. The distance seemed miles, as if we were forced to run through the whole state of Kansas.

With faces set and pain roaring in our heads we ran on. Weak victims of derision and disaster, we were still strong in endurance of pain.

A flat stone ricocheted from the bleeding shoulders of one young runner and struck another. The rustics yelled with delight.

"I'll bet you can't bounce one off their heads," one of them in mud-stained overalls yelled.

"I'll bet I kin," was the answer. The second man ran along throwing rocks.

A rope was stretched across the gantlet. Some jumped it, others rolled under, and others dashed against it. The impact of running bodies upon the hemp sprawled the hay tossers on the ground.

They rose in anger and blasphemy.

A rock crashed into the cadaverous vagrant's eye. It closed, blue and swollen, as suddenly as if a curtain had been pulled over it. A whip hissed around his middle. Another long lash tied about his neck and pulled him to the ground.

Blink jerked the whip from about the sick man's neck amid a hail of stones and clubs. He lifted him up. The vagrant, now blind in one eye, started to run out of the gantlet. A fist crashed into his other eye.

"Damn your yap hearts," he screamed.

He stumbled and fell to his knees. Moaning, his hands tore at his aching and swollen eyes.

A lion's heart beat in his vagabond body. Blind as justice, he managed to stagger, with feet apart, erect. "Come on, you rube bastards! I'll eat your God damn hearts for turnips!" he yelled.

They closed in about him and rattled clubs and stones against his wasted body. Manure-stained hands pounded at him. The blood formed around many abrasions. His lips were swollen and large. His long hair, covered with yellow mud, stuck to his head as if it had been dipped in glue.

Battered, unbroken, unsinkable, a half-dead victim in the net of circumstance, he was still strong enough to defy a horde of yokels.

"My God, they'll kill him!" an old tramp screamed. He started to help. The handle of a scythe cracked across his ankle. His leg doubled like a jackknife under him.

Four of us shouldered our way to the courageous and cadaverous lunger. A blind mass of bleeding and puffed pulp, his fits lashed unknowingly at us.

I jerked his head downward and yelled in his ear.

"We're your pals—we'll get you out of this—come on! A fist caught me in the back of the neck and crashed my head against the lunger's.

Blink grabbed his one arm, I another. Two other vagabonds cleared the way as much as possible.

Once in the open, we made a pocket in which he could run. His ears were raw and puffed. His nose was flat and bloody against his face. A gullied scar ran across his forehead.

Tequila affects the heart for days after a debauch like no other liquor. But still he ran.

Coatless, hatless, with bleeding, raw, and aching bodies, we stumbled and staggered out of reach of our persecutors. The cadaverous rover was far in the lead.

The rain began to pour in torrents.

Exhausted, we reached an enclosure made of rotten railroad ties. The roof was composed of box-car doors crudely spiked together. Warped by the sun and decayed by time, it was only a sieve through which the rain poured.

We huddled near the sides of this enclosure.

The wind-driven rain whistled over the withered weeds and grass. The sky was the color of wet slate, a dismal black-gray. Water dripped everywhere. It turned red and fell from our naked shoulders. A forlorn and bedraggled gathering of vagabonds, we smiled even more forlornly at a ruffian who attempted to start a fire.

He struck wet matches against wet wood. He then patted his naked breast to keep the blood flowing. Others followed his example.

The rain rattled more heavily on the sievelike roof. It gathered in the footprints of animals in the mud. Dead leaves were plastered to the ground.

The air turned much colder.

The rain turned to hail.

It fell clear and hard as crystals; the wind whistled more sharply.

An ancient cottonwood crashed near the enclosure, as though cut to the ground with silver bullets.

A rift of blue shone momentarily in the dismal gray welter.

Dejected and half-naked rascals all, we looked upward as though it were a road in paradise.

"That means it'll rain a month—blue through hail —that's what," a shivering hobo volunteered.

"I wonder if them two old bums that fainted are layin' out in the rain yit," said another.

"No," sneered a third. "The yaps brought 'em umbrellars. They always do that. Why, there ain't nothin' kinder hearted than a yap, 'less it's two yaps."

"Blue through hail," again put in the shivering vagabond. "It done that way the time o' the Big Flood. The Lord, he stood in his gum boots an' says to Moses: 'Bring Noaher in outta the wet—he'll git the anermals damp.' "

"Gosh, you're funny," a voice croaked.

"I may not be funny, but I kin tell when it's goin' to rain a month."

The cadaverous man weakly attempted to push a wet hand through wet, mud-plastered hair. He gasped. "I'd like to know who the hell sent me out to see the world in the rain." He coughed violently.

"Back to Arizona fer you, 'bo," the bedraggled weather prognosticator said. "God's a-callin' another one of his tired hoboes home." Another chortled, "You ain't goin' to see nothin' fer a long time, 'bo. Don't you worry none 'bout that." A gust of wind drowned his words to a dreary cadence.

The hail clattered fiercely on the roof.

"If I ever git to where the sun shines I'll never leave," the cadaverous derelict grunted between fits of coughing. "I won't die shiverin' like a drowned rat, anyhow."

"Well, if you'll jist be patient, boys, I'll drive to the clothin' store in my limmyzine an' bring you all nice new fur coats and silk nighties. I know you boys are cold." An old beggar's mouth twisted in a tooth-less, sardonic grin.

"Who do you think you're kiddin'?" a voice asked irritably.

"Nobody—but the next time somebody wants to

kill Arizona Slim, I wish to Gawd they'd do it while I'm takin' my vacation at Monte Carlo."

The cadaverous men turned closed eyes toward the speaker and coughed again. He held clawlike hands to his heaving, naked chest. Lacerated by life, and torn with suffering, his face was now a mass of wrinkles and wounds.

"I think I'll lay down," he half coughed, "I can't stand it no more."

The water sloshed between his shoulders as he stretched out on the wet ground. For a moment he lay with mouth wide open. Then he tried to sit up. There followed a sound as though water gurgled in his throat. He clutched his thin neck as if to keep the last breath from escaping. His bony hands went downward. His body stiffened. His heels struck the ground twice. Then he lay still.

Pity strangled the lowest rascal into silence. Not a man moved for a moment. With puffed lips, black-and-blue eyes, and bloody bodies, they stood with reverence profound.

A monstrous proof of the innate brutality of man, his so-called brother, the dead lunger resembled an ogre, distorted, horrible, nauseating.

The hurt of life surged in my heart. I gripped Blink's arm.

The hail peltered. A far-away engine shrieked.

"What a hell of a way to die," said Blink with heavy heart.

His words broke the tension.

"What's the difference? You kin see his soul goin' over there now." A withered derelict pointed to a wisp of low cloud through which the hail fell. All looked at the cloud.

"He was goin' to croak where the sun shines—that's how much he *knew*," sneered the weather prognosticator. "He croaked where his beloved Saviour wanted him to croak—that's what."

"Maybe he'll meet Arizoner Slim an' git a coat to face Jesus in. He can't git in heaven lookin' that way," decided the derelict who had pointed at the cloud.

"Jesus'll take him in any old way—he was jist a hobo like us," said a dour fellow who had not spoken before. Hair covered his breast, shoulders, and arms completely. Drops of bloody water stood, like glycerine, all over him.

"Well, Jesus never run into no Sappin' Day," was the cloud pointer's rejoinder.

"The hell he didn't," the dour vagrant retorted quickly. "He died among thieves like him layin' here."

He looked at the dead man's shoes. "His kicks are better'n mine."

He removed them swiftly.

A worn dollar bill fell from between the leather

and lining of the left shoe. Five hands reached for the money. The weather prognosticator clutched it.

The other rascals stood about, nervous as sea gulls over food that had vanished.

"Come on—divvy up," demanded several.

"What do you want me to do—tear it in little pieces?" He pocketed the money defiantly.

The hail ceased. The wind subsided. The sun filtered through clouds that scurried.

"We gotta lot o' coats to bum; we better beat it," someone suggested.

A mendicant looked ruefully at the dead wastrel.

"We hadden oughta leave him here." The words were said dolefully.

"What do you mean—leave him here? Do you wanta build a monurement over him? He's dead, *ain't he?*"

A river to the east could be heard surging with swollen water.

Far above us the buzzards sailed in gyrations of beauty.

Without further parley we left the enclosure and walked under the shining sun.

I lagged behind with Blink.

"Let's beat it from these guys over to the Mexican section—they'll give us clothes."

Arrayed like scarecrows in Mexican cast-off clothing, we hurried westward with the speed of those who pay first-class fares.

In two days we reached a well-known Western jungle.

Two bindle stiffs and a youth my own age sat near a slow fire. A wind rattled sand against battered rusty cooking utensils.

The bindle stiffs were taciturn. Their blankets were rolled in bundles and tied with rope. Phlegmatic, they sat on the ground, elbows on knees, labor-twisted hands clasped, while I exchanged news of the road with the youth. He spoke with a soft Southern accent.

I looked about the jungle with dismal foreboding.

"This doesn't seem right," I said to Blink.

He made no comment.

But still I was uneasy. A deserted jungle usually meant a recent raid by the police.

Worn from hardship, we soon fell asleep. We were awakened by the crashing of clubs against the soles of our shoes.

Policemen stood over us. The bindle stiffs were gone. The youth remained.

"Havin' a little snooze, huh?" one policeman asked. We tried to stand erect.

"Come along with us."

Anxious for freedom, we tried to explain.

"Tell it to the judge—we ain't got time to listen —picked up twenty o' you bums here yesterday."

We stood between our captors on a dingy street corner until the patrol wagon came.

I had a large knife. One policeman opened it and laid it across the palm of his hand. I knew what the action meant. A blade long enough to reach across his palm would be classed as a concealed weapon.

We were booked under the charge of having no visible means of support and carrying concealed weapons. Only our youth, or the deep understanding of the judge would save us from prison.

Handcuffed we stood, a trinity of youth before the dispenser of justice. He had a round soft face and narrow eyes.

He looked at us and then at the police. An officer told his story. I had a concealed weapon. We were hoboes.

The judge listened with no more concern than if we were stray animals. He asked no questions. Fingering a wooden gavel, he said indifferently: "One hundred and twenty days each."

A feeling of overwhelming despair came over me. It was followed by a sense of hurt pride and shame.

A county jail is often more dreaded by hoboes than a penitentiary. "A hundred and twenty days . . ." I counted the months ahead.

Defiance choked a sob in my throat. I wanted to

say something to the judge. But I remembered an underworld admonition: "Never talk to his nibs."

Emotional by nature, but a self-taught stoic, Blink stared expressionless at the judge. The boy from the South gazed at the shining handcuffs which held us together.

There was a lost look in his eyes. It was the same expression I had seen in the eyes of little boys during their first day at the Orphanage. I was to see it later in the eyes of men on gallows. It was as if an inarticulate chaos struggled to be heard.

The boy's eyes took me away from myself. I wanted to protect him. I could feel his arm trembling. I patted his hand.

The words came sharply, "Let's go!"

We were taken to the jail.

CHAPTER II

JAILBIRDS

The jail room was thirty-five feet long, twenty-five feet wide, and seven feet high. In this large cage were fifty prisoners. Some had been sentenced and were serving jail terms; others awaited trial or removal to the penitentiary.

The floor was of thick sheet metal. Around the walls and ceilings were heavy iron bars, painted a ghastly yellow. On each side of the cage was a row of cells, a dozen in all. Each cell was about five by six feet. There were four hammocks in each, one above the other, two on each side. Each hammock contained a filthy blanket.

The veteran inmates had the choice of blankets and hammocks. The prisoner in jail the longest time was the court of last appeal in all disputes.

In case of his release, to go to the penitentiary—or freedom, the next in order took his place.

Between the rows of cells was a long pine table. A bench was on each side of it. There was room for only sixteen men on the benches.

Cards were not allowed in the jail, but there was always a game in progress. Cigarettes, cigars, and plugs of chewing tobacco were the stakes.

Each prisoner, upon his arrival, had been deprived of all his possessions, with the exception of tobacco and handkerchiefs.

The daily routine began at five o'clock in the morning.

A guard awoke us by pounding on the steel bars with an iron weight.

There arose from hammocks, benches, table, and floor as disheveled and terrible a group as ever pleaded for justice before merciless judges.

Swollen from sleep and grim from life, each face was a study for a philosophical misanthrope.

The odor of unwashed bodies was accentuated by the complete lack of ventilation.

There was but one faucet, and at it fifty men washed their faces. We pushed each other out of line like free citizens boarding street cars.

The senior prisoner was allowed to keep a safety razor. He would shave any of his brothers in misery for the equivalent of fifty cents in cigarettes or tobacco. He plied his trade with the grimness of an executioner.

The blade was duller than a sergeant of police. The water was cold. The only soap available was a cake of coarse yellow naphtha. The operation was violent and bloody.

At five-thirty we were called to breakfast. Half the men had not had a chance to wash.

We stood, two by two, at a steel door which opened into another tank, in which was a long pine table.

Steaming hot chicory in a tin cup, two slices of hard bread, a spoonful of hash, and a raw onion made all unhappy for the day.

Ten minutes were allowed in which to eat. It was impossible to gulp the boiling chicory in that time.

While the prisoners breakfasted trusties swabbed the cells. We returned to wet floors and the same odors.

Any cigarettes or trinkets accidentally left in the cells were gone—stolen by the trusties.

Old magazines and daily newspapers strayed into the jail. Every line was read.

If a prisoner had arrived since the preceding morning he was tried immediately after breakfast by a Kangaroo Court.

The charge was that of breaking into the jail without the consent of the inmates. As in the outside world, judge, lawyers, and jury took their places in the curriculum of injustice.

The blindfolded prisoner was led before the assembly. The senior prisoner, who was the judge, subjected him to a series of questions.

What was his age? What was he in for? Would he have an auburn or a brunette maiden to ease the loneliness of prison? Did he have dandruff—or any of the nameless diseases? Would he desire his breakfast brought to him by the chosen maiden as he lolled in bed? Would he have his chosen maiden bow legged or pigeon toed, or both? Or did he prefer a youthful virgin with a darker skin?

When the poor devil tried to name his preference he was told to "shut up." A roar of mocking laughter followed.

He was then given his instructions and told the rules of the prison. The violation of those rules would mean the infliction of so many lashes with a leather belt from the hands of the senior prisoner.

He was then placed upon a blanket in the center of the room. Suddenly the blanket was jerked from under his feet. He sprawled, still blindfolded, upon the floor.

Never was a more moronic entertainment offered in American lodges. After he had nursed his bruises the bandage was removed from the new arrival's eyes. He was "one of the bunch."

If a prisoner offered resistance to the Kangaroo Court he was given the "silence." No one talked to him during the day.

The following morning he was called before the

court again. If he still offered resistance he was given the "silence" again until at last he bowed to the majesty of prison law.

Few men were recalcitrant more than one day.

The prison inmates did not offer to subject two men to the mockery of a Kangaroo Court.

They were Brother Jonathon, an ancient medicine faker, and Nitro Dugan, a yegg of vast dimensions.

Brother Jonathon looked about our tawdry surroundings with a bored smile.

He was visited by a notorious criminal attorney each day.

"Strange are the meanderings of injustice," he said. "I have never known a lawyer who was not a pickpocket at heart—and yet, honest men like myself are forced to engage them. Woe, woe, is my heavily laden soul—the lowest gentleman among us here— even Dippy, the pyromaniac, would have adorned the Supreme Court like a fat oyster had the luck of environment been a force in his youth.

"Lawyers adorn murder with platitudes and eat twisted lies for breakfast . . . they are leaders in the great American march of hypocrisy."

He would walk about in deep thought, his frock coat carefully buttoned, his head bowed, like a tent show evangelist in prayer.

Nitro Dugan was a bark from another tree. He was strong bodied, strong willed, a throwback to far-gone centuries. A barbarian with the gift of mockery, he had hatred of his kind.

He was now in jail on a charge of complicity in the murder of a marshal and robbing a safe. Tiger Spangler, a noted yegg, was sentenced to life for his part in the crime.

Dugan had swaggered into the courtroom, debonair, a silk 'kerchief blazing carelessly from a tailored coat. With a fake alibi and a smile, he had clogged the so-called wheels of justice. The jury had disagreed.

"I'm too big a picture for those saps to frame— I'll beat 'em yet."

A man with the energy and the nature of a tiger, he paced the prison room hour after hour.

Guards brought in and took out different prisoners from early morning until late at night.

Some would leave to face juries of their uncaught peers amid the good wishes and sneers of the other prisoners.

Only the clanking of the iron doors and the calling of convict names by guards and trusties broke the monotony.

The next meal was at two o'clock. Chicory, bread, stew, or beans. We would have no more food that day.

A huge, gorilla-like Negro was the comedian of our

tank. His crooked black arms hung to his knees. His lips were the size of doughnuts cut in half.

He had been released from the penitentiary four months before. After serving ten years as a two-time loser he was now sentenced again for burglary. He laughed from morning until night.

"I'se a bad niggah, I is! 'Tain't no use lettin' dis niggah free no moah, nohow. I jist go percolatin' 'round wit' a gat an' gits in trouble agin. I'se too bad a niggah to be loose exceptin' on a chain."

His eyes glistening with mirthful tears, he would laugh at his monstrous joke.

"I jist do a little burglin', an', hot damn, de cops git me! An' now dey takes dis heah niggah back home to de Big House agin." He would laugh again, louder than before, his great lips shaking.

All in the jail were friendly toward the Negro except the boy from the South.

Dippy, the pyromaniac, was a tall thin ghost of a man touching the shores of fifty. His eyes were blank, his mouth open. He faced a twenty year sentence for arson. His gray hair straggled over a scar on his forehead. One shoulder drooped. One leg was shorter than the other.

He shuffled like a man paralyzed.

The ends of his fingers were blistered from holding burning matches. His eyes followed every match that lit a cigarette or pipe, in the hands of other prisoners. He did not smoke. He would hold the burning piece of wood beneath his fingers. The blaze was lost in the blistered flesh. Prisoners would give him matches just to watch him sit in the corner and strike them on the floor.

Dippy's face was always clouded with gloom save when he watched a burning match. It then became beatified. Over it danced shadows of joy like gleams of sunlight across a shaded, ugly pool. As the blaze burned into nothing his face became dark.

Brother Jonathon was deeply interested in him. The magnificent quack had a pair of eyes that saw beneath the veneer of life. He often talked to Dippy.

With his hands behind his back he would gaze at the pyromaniac kindly and taunt him.

"Oh, Dippy my boy, you would puzzle the Wise Men of the East."

The medicine faker's head went from side to side.

"Queer are the workings of the All Ruler—more things in heaven and earth, Horatio, than are dreamt of in thy philosophy. Queer, queer, passing queer."

Oblivious of jail and the bedraggled lover of blazes in front of him, the old man stood with eyes cast down as though looking into an empty grave.

He remained standing while the pyromaniac ambled slowly away.

Each hour was livened by a song from the Negro.

"Standin' on Fo'th Street,
Lookin' up Main,
Cop come along
An' ask me mah name.

"I tol' him mah name
It was Dennis.McGee
I got seben wil' wimmen
A-workin' foh me.

"Ashes to ashes
An' dus' to dus'
Was dey eber a woman
A burglah could trus'?"

A group would soon gather around him. To the stamping of feet and clapping of hands the Negro would sing:

"He took her to de tailah shop
To have her mouf made small
She swallowed up de tailah
De tailah shop an' all.

"Massa had no hooks an' nails
Nor anything like dat,
So on dis darky's nose he used
To hang his coat an' hat.

"Ashes to ashes
An' dus' to dus'
Was dey eber a woman
A burglah could trus'?

"Toodledum, toodledum,
Ain't we got fun
Hie-ay-hi-oh,
I'm jist a black hobo——"

Then quaintly with facial gestures and pantomime
he would drawl:

"On Monday Ah was arrested,
On Tuesday Ah was tried,
On Wednesday Ah was hung
An' on Thursday—Ah died.

"On Friday Ah wen' to heaben
An' Petah says, 'Oh well,
You packs youh clothes to-morrow
An' go right down to hell.'

"An' den Ah says, 'No, nebah,
Fo' dat would not be faih,
I'se jist a hung dead rascal
An' dey's a lotta p'lice down theah.

" 'I wants to stay in heaven
Because mah neck am soah
An' if I go wheah it's too hot
It'll huht me moah an' moah.

" 'So listen, Blessed Petah,
An' tuhn youh head away
'Cause I'se a hung dead niggah
Who nevah fohgot to pray.'

"So Petah says, 'Deah comrade,
Who was so steep' in sin
Ah'll let you stay in heaben
Fo' a quaht o' niggah gin.'

"An' he took a mop an' bucket
An' washed my soul all white,
An' gimme a bran' new rope
So I could sleep all night."

This song was repeated again and again. It softened the hardest face with smiles. Before the smiles were covered with shadows of reality the huge black would chant:

"Ah loves to be in prison
'Cause I foun' Jesus theah . . ."

He would clap his hands and patter the broad soles of his shoes on the floor as the gathering would join in:

> *"Jesus loves me, yes I know*
> *For the Bible tells me so.*
> *Everything here is done to please us*
> *An' so we're very much obliged to Jesus."*

Suddenly the Negro would sing with quicker tempo:

> *" 'Twas preach' by Paul an' Petah,*
> *They spread it wide an' free,*
> *'Twas hell fo' ol' John Bunyan,*
> *An' it's hell enough fo' me."*

It was as if the happy black had given a wine of gusto to all in the prison.

They followed him lustily and swiftly. Always the Negro's rich voice could be heard above the rest. A moron sinner without conscious sin, a spreader of fear at night and joy by day, he started each verse with the lift of a huge hand, pale yellow inside:

> *"Oh, it don' matter what they preach,*
> *Of high or low degree,*
> *For the old hell of the Bible,*
> *Is hell enough for me.*

"I can't say where the hell it is;
  Or when it will git me,
  But the old hell of the Bible
  Is hell enough for me.

"It may be hot as blazes
  An' scorch my stingaree,
  But the old hell of the Bible
  Is hell enough for me.

"It may be cold as eunicks,
  Attendin' a whore-house tea,
  But the old hell of the Bible
  Is hell enough for me.

"It may be like the jail inside—
  With guards for compan-ee
  But the old hell of the Bible
  Is hell enough for me.

"It may have preachers in it,
  Where they didn't mean to be,
  But the old hell of the Bible
  Is hell enough for me.

"So I thank God an' Jesus
  For teachin' me to see,
  That the old hell of the Bible
  Is hell enough for me."

"Cut out that sacrilege. Ain't you got no respect for nothin'?" a guard asked.

The crowd became silent.

"Jesus died for guys like you—don't you forgit that."

A squeaky voice in the rear said, "That's been so long ago it don't count."

The jailbirds tittered.

The guard frowned. "Who the God damned hell said that—you ungrateful bunch of lousy bastards?"

Silence followed. The defender of the crucified carpenter went on his irate way.

An inmate stopped him with the complaint that his comb had been stolen.

"Well, for Christ's sake!" exclaimed the guard. "Do you think you're in church? Steal the next guy's comb the first chance you git. These guys ain't in here for knittin' socks—don't be a muttonhead all your life."

As the guard closed the iron door the Negro burglar and his associates sang:

> "*The heathen in his blindness*
> *Bows down to wood and stone!*
> *Shall we, whose souls are lighted*
> *With wisdom from on high,*
> *Shall we, to them benighted,*
> *The lamp of life deny?*"

The last two lines were repeated with much fervor.

A conglomerate gathering of frayed rascals, they were completely detached from the outside world. Regardless of color, innocence or guilt, we fraternized one with the other. Some tried to keep hearts from breaking; others tried only to kill the monotony of the hours. Thrown together by the steel bars of circumstance, we snarled, quarreled, and cursed. Many seemed to bear all other burdens easier than propinquity.

One man among them held himself aloof.

Accused of forgery, with the certainty of conviction and a long term, he walked nervously up and down the tank. Even in misery he made no comradeship with more illiterate and braver rascals. His body was taut, his eyes swollen and strained at a door that did not open—for him.

Slowly the madness came upon him. Each night he wept and groaned. He may as well have thrown particles of ice at the sun.

Each time the iron door clanged he would suddenly rush forward and exclaim, "Yes, sir! I'm ready."

All but the pyromaniac and Brother Jonathon would laugh.

The door would let another prisoner out or in— and clang shut.

The forger would stand transfixed for a moment and gaze at the iron-gray door.

At last it opened for him.

One trusty took his head, another his feet. He was hurried out one morning with a leather strap around a swollen purple throat—a suicide.

The Negro laughed as he told his decrepit mates: "He'll git up to heaven, and de good Lawd, He'll say, 'What fo' you done fohged mah name fo'? I'se goin' to put you to writin' down de names ob de preachahs an' judges who keeps comin' to hell for-ebeh an' ebeh.'"

A trusty brought in a paper which contained a picture of the forger's wife and daughter. The young girl was posed by the photographer so as to display her beautiful legs. Her picture was fastened to the wall.

Otherwise life went on in the prison as though the forger had not lived among men who knew neither dawn nor dusk.

Electric lights burned by day. At night all of them save a dim bulb over the door were switched out.

The pyromaniac would sit on his hammock and burn a last match before going to sleep.

At intervals in the night the main lights were turned on—then off. The door clanged open and shut. A new face appeared in the morning.

Dope fiends, eaten with disease, were always well supplied with "snow." The guards either knew or feigned ignorance for money. The prisoners knew. A stool pigeon told a guard. No action was taken.

Friends regularly brought them clean handkerchiefs. The hems contained cocaine. A spot soaked in morphine would be marked with a lead pencil. The saturated cloth would be soaked in a spoon of water. A match under the spoon, a safety pin jabbed into the arm—dreams again.

Hypo Sleigh was the shrewdest of the dope fiends.

Tobacco smoke circled heavy as fog about the steel room.

Men paced up and down, up and down, like automatons on a wire stretched across the empty chasm of life. It was night always—with never a ray of day in the jail, or in our hearts. The Negro burglar alone was happy.

After many days the monotonous hum of voices would tell on our nerves. We ached for solitude away from iron bars and caged men.

Each night a trusty came with a large can of Epsom salts. Coarse food, no exercise, bad air, and overwrought nerves made indigestion king.

Ignorance and false pride sustained the inmates. Pride and hope. Alone, they might have given way to tears.

The Negro hoped for chicken again—in fifteen years.

Minds dulled with too much revery, with too much smoking, too many incessant tunes, often took on the illusion that they had always been behind the bars.

Among the two- or three-time losers there was always much talk. Notes were compared. Denver Shorty, Texas Gyp, and Gimp the Red, each with a coterie of friends about him, talked of robbed banks and bullets in the night. Young first offenders, actuated by the ego that makes the King and the yegg twin brothers, listened with awe.

"I blazed it out with the rube constable and heard him fall in the alley. Another yap threw a bullet against the wall in back o' me. We got away with twenty grand—but Davenport Pete fell. A rube district attorney took three thousand an' got him off with a little rap of a year. We sprung him in ten months. . . ."

And Denver Shorty called, "Ain't that so, Gimp?"

Gimp answered, "Yeah—what is it?"

In this world of iron bars and dim lights ego paraded with braggadocio. Many lies were told.

"My kid brother's only twelve years old, but he's the best thief you ever saw," was Texas Gyp's contribution.

Young lads, never before in jail, told tales of long incarcerations for desperate crimes. Like snobs the world over, they wished to edge into the society which they admired.

Two brothers were in for automobile stealing. The younger, not over eighteen, was taken out of jail one morning at nine o'clock.

The older brother walked the jail, mumbling, "If those cops are givin' the kid the third degree I'll kill 'em."

A guard brought the boy into the jail that afternoon. His face was black and blue. He staggered from exhaustion.

Ferocious hulks of life gathered about guard and boy. Among them was the brother. The guard, to whom the boy had been delivered by the police, now met a heavy fist with his jaw.

The guard's head dropped sideways as though his neck had snapped. With leopard speed Nitro Dugan crashed a fist low at his bending stomach.

He sank, silent.

A riot started. Other guards took their comrade out of the tank. The young criminal's brother was knocked unconscious with a blackjack and dragged out of the door. He died next day in a hospital.

The younger brother, after bleeding and groaning all night, was taken away in an ambulance.

Added to the charge of stealing against him was the new one of resisting an officer.

The trusties were really the rulers of our little world. Their unpaid services added to the graft of the jailer. Like others of that kind, they assumed great dignity with their little authority.

Prisoners serving jail sentences, they had privileges. They could run errands. They had ample time to eat their meals. They were given as much food as they liked. Nonentities in the outer world, they were despots in a shut-away wilderness of iron.

Many of them were reluctant to leave when their terms expired. One had been a trusty at alternating periods for forty years. Old, hopeless, broken, derelict, he would purposely commit small crimes in order to reënter the jail and become a trusty again.

He had never been in the Big House, or penitentiary. He scorned all those who had. Like most criminals, petty and great, he was really a moron moralist at heart.

Nearing seventy, bent double, with an awful leer on his face, he was known to us as Old Crow. Intensely a Christian, he pored over his Bible with fanatical eyes. As bitter as St. Paul, and meaner in heart than Calvin, life had put glue on his fingers.

They stuck to everything.

A stool pigeon, he told everything to the guards —stole everything from the men.

Youths facing the state penitentiary the first time eagerly asked him questions about the Big House. Always loquacious, he told them between sneers of the hard way of crime.

A newcomer slept in a heroin stupor.

There was blood on his hands and clothes. The morning paper came. A man was dead.

This was the murderer. The prisoners stared at his neck in silence.

He slept peacefully in the last moments of untroubled oblivion he was ever to have.

His hat was on the floor beside him. His shirt was torn to the belt. His collar was gone. His four-in-hand scarf was in a hard knot, as though a hand had pulled it tight.

He did not remember the quarrel.

A clean-shaven fellow had been brought into the jail with the murderer. His eyes were furtive and rheumy. His manner was a conciliatory apology. He told with weak gusto of being caught in the attempt to rob with a deadly weapon. He established himself on terms of familiarity with everybody in the jail. But the two-time losers, with an air of suspicion, withdrew from him.

"They got 'im in here to pump the guy that bumped the fellow off. Then they'll use it agin him at the trial," was Gimp the Red's comment.

It went around the jail, like gossip at a woman's club. The new arrival was a stool pigeon.

Nitro Dugan, Gimp the Red, and Denver Shorty were in the washroom with a dozen other prisoners.

The loquacious fellow with the furtive eyes was among them.

There was a sudden groan. A fist crashed at the base of his brain. His eyes went tight shut with pain. Blows whistling with sudden speed smashed his face and body. A foot caught him in the groin. Bleeding, twisted, groaning, he writhed on the slippery floor.

The prisoners regained composure and washed themselves in the nonchalant manner of men at a hunting club.

A guard came, asked many questions, made many threats.

No one seemed to know who hit the stool pigeon.

The bleeding mongrel was taken away.

The prisoners went without breakfast that morning.

The old plan of the police to have one criminal win another's confidence and betray him had been frustrated.

A few days later the murderer returned from the courtroom. In his ears still rang, "To be hung by the neck until you are dead, and may God have mercy on your soul!"

His hands, in steel bracelets, were before him. His eyes stared, unseeing.

The handcuffs were removed. His cell door was closed. The guard left.

He fell wearily to his cot. His head sagged low.

As if unable to hold it up, he placed his elbows on his knees and rested his jaw in the palms of his hands.

Only the pyromaniac noticed him.

He looked at the bent-over figure for several minutes. Walking to his cell door he asked, "Have you got a match?"

The man lifted his furrowed face. "Yes."

He rose unsteadily and handed the pyromaniac a small box of matches.

The incendiary's eyes glowed.

"Thanks—thanks!" And then, "It is all over?"

"Yeah—I drew the rope. They're stretchin' it now, I suppose."

The pyromaniac lit a match. It burned into his fingers while he watched.

"Well, it don't make much difference," he finally said. "Everybody kicks the bucket sooner or later."

The condemned man rolled a cigarette. The pyromaniac held a match for him. He watched the blaze while the murderer smoked feverishly.

"You know," he said, lighting another match, "I wouldn't be afraid to die. I'd rather like it. I wish this place'd burn up now."

"But I'd want the judge in it," snapped the murderer, "and that damn pie-faced jury. I raved in my sleep last night at the hangman—he painted my neck white where it was swollen an' purple, an' he put me in an iron coffin an' gave me a hammer, sayin', 'Here, pal, you kin pound your way out.' They dropped me through the trap—and I laughed and wriggled my way outta the rope." He felt his throat. "I wish to God it was over."

"It don't take long," said the pyromaniac. "Not over a minute."

"No, it's the waitin' that kills. I gave the guy I bumped a better deal. He only died *once*."

"O' course you'll have a preacher at the last," suggested the pyromaniac.

"If they send me a preacher they'll hang me twice," was the answer.

Over his face passed clouds of reality.

"But, Bralen," continued the pyromaniac, "it wouldn't do no good to have the judge and jury die. They'd just get others."

The murderer looked at the incendiary between puffs of smoke.

"Besides, you shouldn't feel that way about 'em. They hain't no worse'n us—just different."

He struck another match.

"If you die feelin' happy toward everybody you'll wake up in t'other world with your soul clean like fire."

"Maybe you're right," answered the man about to die.

The incendiary walked to a group of prisoners.

"Bralen got the rope," he said.

The pyromaniac turned to Nitro Dugan.

"They're goin' to pop Bralen's neck!"

The desperado looked at the lighter of flames. Dippy hurried away with the news of Bralen's coming death. Dugan sauntered toward the condemned man.

"So you drew the rope—eh, mate? Well—we're all under sentence of death. Take it standing up, kid. They'll tie your ankles together anyhow—and they'll hang you even if you bend like an empty sack. They've got no more mercy than God!"

Bralen stood erect and looked in the yegg's eyes. Massive men were they both.

"You'll meet a lot of people I know, Bralen. They're all in hell. If you see One Eyed Daley—the old-time warden, show him a glass of water. Tell him it's from me. My gift to his burning tongue. Jerk it back when he's about to grab it—then throw more fire in his eyes. God damn him!" He laughed loudly. "All the men who've been hung you'll find over in a corner. They won't associate with the other people down there because they died for their sins on earth."

Bralen turned his eyes away.

Dugan continued: "I'll tell you how to beat the game—jump when they spring the trap. That way you'll commit suicide and they'll think they hung you. Eddie Wilson did that and laughed at 'em in his coffin. He died over a broad, too. Ho—ho—God Almighty! Hell's crowded with men who died for women. If they keep on there won't be any room for the wardens and the guards."

Bralen looked at the floor. Dugan turned his eyes to the open door which allowed another prisoner to enter.

It was evening.

The Negro was starting for the penitentiary. He sang like one going on a glorious adventure.

> *"Hang up de fiddle an' de bow,*
> *Lay down de shobel an' de hoe,*
> *Dey's no moah stealin' fo' pooh ol' Ned,*
> *He's goin' wheah de bad niggahs go."*

He walked about getting ready, an antediluvian monster with the gift of laughter, his doughnut-lipped mouth open from ear to ear.

With crooked short legs, gigantic chest, and baggy green-striped pants, the frayed bottoms of which dragged on the floor, and with a colorless shirt that was grimy and torn, he faced the meaningless futility of his chaotic life with the laughter of a fool.

The fat guard waited, his hard lower lip and undershot jaw twisted in a smile at the Negro.

"Come on here, Rastus—time to go. They can't wait your Pullman all night, you know."

"Dat's all right, Mistah Guard. Tell 'em fo' me dat Alexander Hamilton Jones'll be comin' right along, an' tell none o' dem boys to come to de train to meet me, 'cause I'se been deah befoah."

His eyes turned to the murderer's cell.

"Ah'll be waitin' fo' you, boy."

"Go on, you black devil—an' chew on a bone like an ape!"

The Negro laughed louder than ever.

"Jis' heah dat white boy talk! You bettah jis' say all you kin, 'cause dey's goin' to buhn youah neck till it pops an' make it all red."

The murderer stood up, his hands gripping the cell door until his fingers were white.

His heavy lantern jaw was hard set. He scowled at the Negro. The Negro went on:

"Bettah grin a little, white boy—'cause you'se goin' to dance till you knees cave in—an' you bettah pray hahd, too, Mistah Man, 'cause dey's gonna hang you so fast it'll be three days befoah de Lawd knows you'se daid."

"Come on, Rastus," laughed the guard.

The Negro put a shapeless hat on a bullet head and shouted: "So long, eberybody! See you all in jail! Why dey allus takes you away at night so's you cain't see no purty country is moah'n I know."

Guard and convict moved towa.d the door. Another guard entered.

"Bring Bralen," he said.

The murderer's cell was opened. He was handcuffed to the Negro. One smiled. The other frowned.

They marched away.

CHAPTER III

A BOY FROM THE SOUTH

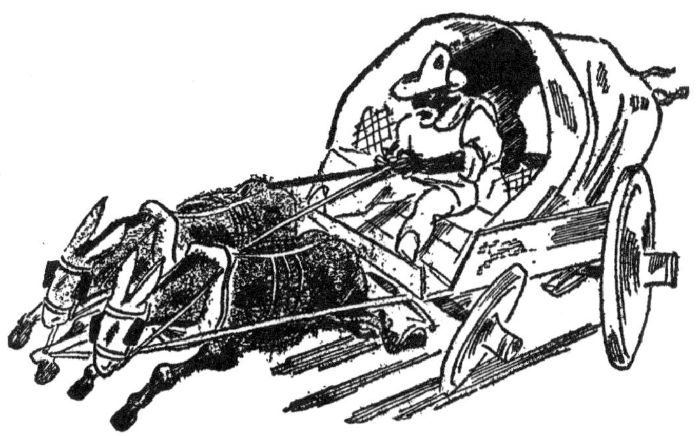

Four of us soon formed a group in the prison —Blink, Eddie Evans, the boy from the South, and I.

The judge who had sentenced us was known as "the nemesis of the hobo." We knew not, at the time, what nemesis meant. We were certain, however, that it signified something terrible.

The judge acquired his reputation in another county.

At that time he would sentence hoboes at any hour of the day or night. The police would ring the bell of his house even at midnight. The light would go on in his bedroom. The window would open.

The judge, not looking out of the window, would ask, "How many have you?"

The reply would indicate the number of vagrants.

"Give them all a hundred and twenty days each."

This sentence early became an obsession with him.

He was known among vagabonds as "Old-hundred-and-twenty-days Crawley."

The judge was given cause one winter night to speculate on the ingratitude of vagabonds. As he opened his window a bullet tore through his left shoulder.

Two officers stood, with eight hoboes, beneath the window. They rushed into the house.

The hoboes hurried away.

The silent avenger was never caught.

This episode made the nemesis of the hobo more bitter. For several years he alternated his sentence of one hundred and twenty days with "six months."

The judge's unknown assailant was condemned everywhere in hoboland. To have missed a legal heart with a bullet was a blunder beyond forgiveness.

"Jist think," snarled an old yegg, "the damn fool had a straight aim—and missed."

"Well, the old devil's heart wasn't very big," his fellow yegg returned.

"That's so—I never thought o' that. But why the hell didn't he aim at his belly?"

"Maybe he didn't wanna hurt his soul."

The retort elicited, "G'wan."

The episode of the bullet helped the judge when later the finger of suspicion pointed at him. The sheriff of the county furnished food for the prisoners. His charge for feeding each convict was a dollar a day.

Every arrest and sentence of one hundred and twenty days was recorded. No record was made of the release. The sheriff continued to charge for the absent convicts' upkeep.

He became wealthy. So did the judge. Both men continued for years as honest public servants.

Impulsive and generous, the boy from the South would give everything he had to the first person who asked. He gave his portion of bread to the convict next to him during his first meal in the jail. He was so gentle in manner that attempts were soon made to impose on him.

His temper was immediately discovered to be so vile that the bravest ruffian refrained from disturbing him further.

When a convict tried to caress him he hit him across the temple with the leg of a stool and knocked him unconscious. When not molested he was the most docile person in the jail. We soon talked of vagabond trails in the South.

In the six months preceding his arrest he had achieved the greatest feat in American vagabondia —he had beaten his way from Maine to California.

The lad from the South showed traces of gentility. I envied his soft enunciation and gentle manners.

"Who taught you to think of everyone else first?" I asked him.

He replied, "My mother."

"Where is she?"

"Dead."

I said no more.

As day followed day he became more ill at ease. Once when I complained of the length of our sentence he said quietly, "I can stand on my head that long." And then with a touch of sadness, "Wait till they hand you a real sentence!"

I wondered at his words, but remained silent.

They took him to the Bertillon room later that morning. He was returned at noon.

A look of agony was in his eyes. His full red lips were moist. He touched them nervously with his tongue.

His face was blanched with terror and wonder.

Perspiration gathered on his forehead. He sucked in his cheeks until deep hollows formed on each side of his face.

He stood before me for a moment and tried to speak. I knew nothing—and everything.

"Come on, kid," I said.

I touched his elbows.

He stepped backward.

"They got me," he said. His shoulders sagged. "I'd rather be dead."

His knees bent for a second. He tried to walk and

failed. I took his arm. Wearily he sat on a pine bench in front of a cell.

He said, almost to himself: "Everything tallied—fingerprints and all. It's ninety-nine years and life besides for me—but maybe I won't have to serve the life stretch after I do the ninety-nine. I'll be a hundred and seventeen—and then I'll do life."

A short distance away Gimp the Red and Denver Shorty argued about how loaded dice were made. The boy tried to smile. Words had choked in his heart for six months. Now there was no longer need of secrecy.

"I should have stayed away from that jungle. I got too fresh. Been everywhere—and two hicks picked me up. Now I've got to go back.

"It was an awful joint. The bloodhounds howled all night. There were over fifty of them—and they could smell one of us a mile off. They hated us even further than that.

"We were fed bread and molasses and beans every meal of every day. On Sunday we got black-jack coffee. It was nothing else but chicory.

"Razor-back hogs as tall as calves would squeal outside for the leavings. Niggers and Mexes and half-insane cons slept with us in rows along the wall —three layers high, one bunk on top of the other.

"There was no air in the place—and all of us in from the cotton fields without bathing—well it stunk so that I put cotton in my nose each night before I could go to sleep.

"We'd have to eat and be out in the cotton fields at dawn. Everywhere you turned you could see a guard with a shotgun. They'd be sitting on their prancing horses, a big leather whip hanging from their saddles.

"They could zip you on the ear with the end of that whip, and then draw it back in such a way that you felt your ear was gone.

"My fingers would ache, and my knuckles would bleed, and my back would hurt until I'd wish to God I was dead.

"I wasn't used to that kind of a life—it came sudden—like everything does with me."

The last words were uttered with a deep sigh.

"The head guard would yell out, 'Number one— cotton field squad.' We'd get in line and they'd count us—then the whole twelve of us would leave. A lot of times there were ten cotton field squads. Then he'd yell for the hoe squads and the plow squads.

"Each squad would start off with its guard to the fields. The plow squads were lucky—they could ride their mules—but we had to drill.

"There used to be an old burglar in my squad. His mouth was so crooked that one end of it nearly touched his nose. He didn't have a forehead at all. If he'd had a brain there'd of been no place for it.

"He always had water on his left kneecap. It made him crippled. He'd spend all his spare time rolling that kneecap around.

"He'd swing his toe at the cotton plant and grin silly and sing:

> " *'It's drill ye tarrier, drill,*
> *It's drill ye tarrier, drill,*
> *It's work all day*
> *Without shugar in your tay*
> *Workin' on the London railway.'*

"Sometimes his knee would pain him so much it darn near made his crooked mouth straight. One time the poor old devil collapsed right on top of a cotton plant.

"The guard came up and put him down for twelve lashes on the bare back that night for *destroying* state property. They took him out for the whipping before dusk.

"The captain came with a tough leather, three feet long and over an inch thick. It had an iron handle big enough for a man's two hands. He couldn't hit hard enough with one hand, I guess.

"Then five guards held Kneecap's hands and legs and head. His back was made bare.

"The niggers would shiver and stare all over the joint whenever there was a whipping.

"No one can tell you what the whippings are like.

You've got to get one to know. It's something like as if your back was burned with fire, then someone put a hotter and hotter poker on it each time.

"You squirm till you can ache no more. Sometimes even the guards can hardly hold an old man, the pain is so much. It just tears your flesh loose.

"After this beating Kneecap nearly died. Then they put him in the 'Pull-do squad.' Their job is to keep it clean around the prison yards. One morning old Kneecap stood about a hundred feet from the brick wall. Without a word he give a run and a jump and butted the top of his head against it. His skull was cracked in two places. He died that night.

"I never felt so glad for anything in my life. Everybody on the prison farm was happy except the guards, and they didn't care.

"We'd be stretched across the cotton field, ten squads of us, hoeing a hundred and two rows of cotton at once. We'd carry our hoes back and forth from headquarters, and if we lost them we'd get it on the back for being careless with state property. We'd pile them along the fence at headquarters after we checked them in.

"A nigger broke his hoe handle and tried to steal mine. I didn't think it was right, me working with niggers anyhow, so I cracked him over the head while I was mad.

"The guard saw me—and I got put in the chains

for twelve hours. They put chains around my wrists that held me up so my toes just barely touched the ground. The backs of my legs ached till they went numb. When they took me down I couldn't stand up for three days, so they put me in a damp, dark cell. And all because a nigger tried to steal my hoe.

"But I didn't care; it was better in the cell than out in the fields . . . and would you believe it, when I got out, that nigger had my hoe.

"I nearly cut his toes off out in the field. The guard came running up and started slashing at me with his whip. I picked up a live rattlesnake and threw it at him. It went wriggling and hissing through the air, and that guard got out of the way like he was the governor. He fell on top of the snake, and his six-shooter went off . . ."

The lad from the South smiled faintly.

"They put me in the dark cell for a week, and when I was good and starved they gave me thirty lashes from my knees to the edge of my neck.

"I was all blood for a long time. I had to sleep on my belly for a month. If I'd roll over ever so little the hurt would wake me. And even now if you press your fingers hard on my back the flesh breaks open. My back hurt so I couldn't bear my shirt to touch it. But I had to get out in the cotton field just the same. After I'd hoe a little while each morning my back would be running sores and my shirt would stick to it at noon when I had lunch. When I'd start hoeing again it would tear the shirt loose. I thought it never would get well.

"Finally one Saturday a con died in the field from sunstroke. He just gasped once and stretched out. It sounded like letting air out of a toy balloon.

"I no sooner saw his eyes popping out of his head than I passed out too. When I come to I was stretched out by the side of the dead con.

"A lot of blue bottle flies were buzzing around his mouth. Some were crawling in and out like it was a cave. We were near the bank of the river, and I could tell by the sun the rest of the squad would be through in about an hour. Then they'd come for us. Some of the squad would have to take turns carrying the dead guy to headquarters where they'd give out word that he croaked of heart disease or something. We were over two miles from headquarters, and it would take the bloodhounds quite a while to get my scent after they got them. I figured it would take them longer if I could swim a little narrow river and put water between us. I knew there were ways to fool bloodhounds.

"There was a barbed wire fence ten feet high between me and the river. If I tried to climb over it a guard would see me; or some con might, if the guard didn't, and give me away—to get a job as trusty himself. So I crawled up and down the fence till I saw an opening between the bottom wire and the ground. Then under the fence I went.

"I thought a mile a minute. I run along the river till I saw where a willow arched away over and almost touched another willow on the other side. I climbed up and jumped from the one branch to the other. The branch on the other tree broke, but I fell on the ground instead of in the water. Then I run like a blind Indian till I came to the road that went to the town. A Mexican kid lived there. He'd been released over seven months before, and I remembered the street and number of his house.

"I couldn't beat it down the open road, for I knew I couldn't go a mile without being turned in. So I stretched out under the bridge near the road and waited for dark.

"I knew if I had to stick where I was too long the hounds might get me, and I knew if I could grab a wagon I could put them off any scent they might have picked up.

"You don't know what it's like till bloodhounds get after you. They come baying over the ground with their ears flapping and their mouths lathering green. And if they get up to you ahead of their keepers they're liable to tear you to pieces.

"Pretty soon I heard the siren blow five times— and then blow three times steady every two minutes. It came dusk and not a rig passed on the road.

"Pretty soon I heard the hounds baying loud as lions, and my heart missed several beats. They kept coming nearer—then their baying stopped. I hoped they'd lost the scent and I breathed deep. They started again louder and nearer than before. The sweat turned cold on me. I thought I saw a hound's eyes glaring at me like a cat's in the dark.

"I darn near cried.

"Then I heard hoofs pounding on the road. A wagon rumbled.

"The sounds came nearer, and I heard the nigger driver singing:

> " *'In the evening by the moonlight,*
> *You could hear dem darkies singin'*
> *In the evening by the moonlight*
> *You could hear dem banjoes ringin' . . .'*

"For a minute it made me think of home and all that happened. The moon was over in the east—big and red as the sun. It all hurt me so much that I cried a little.

"The bloodhounds and the hoofs kept getting nearer, and I made up my mind to ride in the wagon, if I had to kill the driver.

"It was a nigger chicken-peddler's wagon. A lot of chickens were in crates on the side. I jumped in the back and crawled up to the nigger on the seat.

There was nothing to do but take a chance. He could hear the bloodhounds and seeing me would tell him the truth. If he'd try to turn me over I'd choke him if I could, and keep him in the wagon and drive on.

"The bloodhounds were right close to the road when I yelled to the nigger, 'Keep on driving, and don't turn around! We just want to get away—we don't want to kill you.'

"That nigger slapped the lines on the mules' backs so loud it made the bloodhounds quiet for a minute. 'All right, Mistah!" he yelled.

" 'Keep looking right ahead,' I hissed in his ear, 'there's five of us in your wagon—we've all got big guns. Put your hands halfway up—hold the lines and drive like you was going home. Sing a little. . . .'

"The coon started warbling 'In the evening by the moonlight' while I went through his pockets. He had about fifteen dollars.

"I hated to take it all, so I gave him a five dollar bill back.

" 'We're just taking half,' I said to him.

" 'Dat's all right, Mistah—you's kin hab it all if you likes.'

"I couldn't help but pity the poor devil. He was only a nigger huckster, but he'd do anything to save his life.

"I took a blue handkerchief from his hip pocket. It was half as big as a shawl.

" 'Come on here, men—help me!' I shouted.

"I wrapped it around his head, across his eyes. Then I twisted the ends around his neck.

" 'We're not going to hurt you, Nigger. We just don't want you to see where we're going. Just sit real quiet—for if you try to jump from the wagon we'll kill you.'

"The nigger trembled all over. I thought his teeth would chatter out of his head.

"I lit some matches I got from his vest pocket and found a lot of twine in the wagon.

"I made him slow the team down while I traded clothes with him. Then I tied his hands and feet.

"I remember taking the money I'd stolen from him out of my pocket. But I forgot to give him the five dollar bill I'd given back to him. So the poor devil lost all his money, anyhow."

A half-whimsical smile came over the young jailbird's face.

"He must have been a good nigger at that. But I couldn't take any chances."

Regret was in his voice.

"I put him back on the wagon seat and yelled, 'Now sit still and watch him, men—if he makes a move shoot him right through the head and throw him in the ditch!'

" 'Ah'll be quiet—Ah'll be quiet,' the nigger sobbed.

"I must have driven fifty miles. The nigger never

made a move. When I drove through the big town I was heading for I gave up the idea of going to the Mexican kid's house, for I had a hunch they'd go there to look for me, so I went cross country fifty miles off to a town another railroad went through.

"When I come to where a road crossed the far end of the railroad yards I turned the team around. I knew that mules could find their way home like a cat.

"I never said a word to the nigger. I trotted the team and tied the lines to the seat and jumped from the wagon. The team knew they were headed for home. I could tell.

"That's been six months ago, and I've been on the road ever since then. I'd begun to think I was out of danger when they picked me up at that jungle."

The boy from the South sighed and said slowly: "Old Kneecap's got it on me—he's dead. I've got to go back."

His eyes were tragic. He fought back the tears.

"Oh, well," the words came wearily.

"Something may happen—you may get a pardon," I consoled.

"A pardon like Kneecap got. My life is done." The words fell heavily.

"What were you in for?" I asked.

"Murder," was the sudden answer.

And then as suddenly, "I didn't mean to. My

mother was only dead a month. She was fine. She always told my father never to whip me. He never did while she lived. He was awful good when he wasn't mad—just like a big brother.

"But he had a temper like mine. He started to beat me. I killed him before I thought."

In four days an officer appeared to take the boy back to his native state.

He submitted to the handcuffs with a look of despair.

Prisoners gathered around him.

The slow-moving official allowed him to bid us all good-bye.

"So long, kid! So long, kid!" came from many throats.

Joe Elvin, the young murderer, yelled cheerily from his cell, "Good luck, kid—you got a one way ticket on the Dixie Flyer."

The boy from the South looked up.

"Maybe I'll take a stop-over," he returned grimly.

And then more cheerfully to me and Blink, "Good-bye, kids, I'll remember you both."

"So will we," I answered.

"Hell—he won't have time to remember," put in Sailor Burren, who usually had little to say.

The iron door closed. The boy from the South was gone.

CHAPTER IV
VAGABONDS AND THIEVES

Nitro Dugan was a roving yegg. Unlike most of his tribe who spring from the poor, he came from a highly respected Eastern family. He had two sisters as handsome as himself. His mother was gray haired, gentle, cultured. His father was a chemist who died in the early fifties.

In spite of money and influence Dugan was sent to the reform school at seventeen. He remained two years. During this period he grew better looking, harder, more defiant. His nose became aquiline, his forehead higher. His face, cast like William McKinley's, grew more stern. He was Spanish and Irish.

A man reveals more of himself in prison than elsewhere. It is a nerve-torn world, the majority of whose citizens are illiterate and unstable.

The guards, and often the judges, are on the same mental level.

Vengeance, twin brother of ignorance, has always been the spirit which permeates prisons.

Youth learns the way of crime in reform schools and county jails. It emulates men who impress it early.

Dugan was a superior graduate of the reform school. He survived in an environment that would have made cringing weaklings of most men.

His first crime was that of attacking a truant officer. He was arrested and taken before the judge in handcuffs.

Released from the reform school, he attacked the officer again. He was sentenced by the same judge to the same institution. Asked why he had attacked the same man again, he replied, "He let my mother see me in handcuffs."

He knew the nature of explosives better than any yegg in the country.

Nitro was a past master at boiling dynamite in water. He would pour off the water and retain the oily substance which remained at the bottom of the vessel. This was called "grease," or "soup." Nitroglycerin was its proper name. A pint of this solution would blow up a building.

One of Dugan's companions, while drunk, had carelessly thrown a bottle of it upon the ground. There was no funeral.

His pet phrase of contempt for an inefficient yegg was, "He couldn't even rob a sheet iron safe."

Dugan could "unbutton an iron safe and put it to bed" with alacrity.

He dented the reputation of the leading manufacturers of safes in America. He was offered work as an expert by them. He hated all men who work. He called them "saps."

A firm once turned out what was considered an "unbeatable safe." They made the error of adjusting the lock on stereotyped numbers and combinations.

With astounding patience Dugan tried one remembered combination after the other. He robbed the safe.

The firm changed the combination. Dugan went to the town in which the safe was manufactured and stole the number.

After he had once robbed a bank which contained such a safe it was considered an "inside job." An employee was arrested, but later proven innocent. Dugan watched the trial reports with interest.

At twenty he left Boston with all the money he could borrow and steal. His mother and sisters, trained in social lies, no longer mentioned his name out of the family circle. They never saw him again.

His mother died within a year. He read of the

death—and spoke of it but once—ten years later. Dugan was by this time being supported by the middle-aged keeper of a Chicago bawdy house on Michigan Boulevard.

He induced his benefactress to go on a trip around the world with him. Returning to America via Japan, he deserted her in San Francisco. Dugan never explained an action to himself, never rationalized. He seldom talked of his affairs with women. Save that he could not completely efface the early marks of gentility at all times, he was a barbarian.

Proud of the name he had carved in the underworld, he was known before thirty wherever railroads carried vagabonds and thieves.

He appeared in all sections of the country.

The tales of his exploits were many.

No bird flew through the air. No bare branch stirred.

The turbulent water of Lake Huron was icily supine in the midst of the frozen desolation. The little town in the Thunder Bay river section was buried deep in snow. For days the weather had remained the same.

The cold cut to the marrow of sparsely clad bones, like frost-bitten razor blades. The deep drifted snow glinted chameleon-like under the spasmodically shining sun. It, too, seemed a frozen candle in the sky.

All day the wind had whirled the snow in every

direction. It abated by night, and the snow ceased falling. A deadly calm and a deadlier cold settled over the earth. It was twenty degrees below zero.

Every living thing had hunted shelter for the night. The stars glistened above, as if piercing through the atmosphere with swords of burning steel. The moon was a mist of frozen white and yellow.

To keep beggars from freezing the calaboose was left open. A pine structure for the lesser offenders, it stood on a side street—alone.

A group of vagabonds huddled around a jumbo stove in a wretchedly furnished room that faced a row of cells. The window of the room was stuffed with rags; there were but three unbroken panes of glass left. The door was cracked and frostbitten. The unbroken panes were covered with a heavy frost. A large lamp, fastened with a bracket, was above the door.

The echo of a locomotive whistle was heard, like the far-away sound of vibrant music. The vagabonds listened, and a flare of interest passed over their life-beaten and weather-lashed faces. But no word was said as they turned their eyes to the round stove again, like tired dogs dozing. The engine whistled once more, and all eyes became alert.

"That old boy's a ramblin' to git out o' the cold," said a derelict with a wizened face. "He thinks it'll be warmer'n Detroit."

"Yeap," said a one-legged man, "it's a hell of a

night for yeggs and hoboes. I wouldn't even want a railroad bull out on a night like this. We're gittin' punished for our sins."

"It'll be hotter'n this when you *really* git punished fer your sins, One Leg," grunted a heavy man with a red kerchief around his neck.

"Maybe so, maybe so," drawled One Leg. "I been punished enough in my time for all I ever done."

The heavy man, a crumbling mountain of muscle, smiled a crooked smile, rubbed his week-old beard with a knuckle-cracked hand, and said, "What da hell, what da hell—gettin' soft, One Leg? You'd steal pennies from dead men's eyes."

"You bet your life I would, Husky. Dead men dor't need no pennies, and they don't need their eyes shut— they can't see nothin'."

The group laughed without mirth.

"I hope no hobo's on that rattler just pullin' in. He'd freeze—sure's Gawd is just," said the derelict with the wizened face.

"Don't worry your potato soul, Weazle," advised the man called One Leg. "They ain't no smart 'boes ridin' freights to-night. And them that ain't smart— well, the deader the better. Too many dumb ones on the road already."

The decrepit of the earth lapsed into silence. The husky vagabond rose and reached into the bottom of the wood box. He pulled out a chunk of wood. "Don't know what we'll do when the wood's gone," he sneered. "Burn the shack down, I guess."

"I'd just as soon," responded One Leg. "These jails are gettin' rottener every year. A self-respectin' tramp can't stop in them no more. It used to be when I first went on the road they was decent jails. You'd git good eats and java. Now all you git is hell from the jailers and corn bread and chicory."

He was interrupted by the man with the wizened face. "Well, if you don't like the jails you kin quit trampin'." Then, scornfully, "Quit your crabbin'! You're lucky they let the jails open."

The large man moved his shoulder and neck muscles nervously, completely oblivious of the conversation.

"What's the matter, Husky, old snowbird, do you want a shot?" asked a vagabond, looking at him.

"Naw, I don't want a shot. Gosh! Can't a man sit quiet without you mosquitoes buzzin' at him? I was jist thinkin' o' the days I was a man—and a damn good one at that."

"What you was don't buy ham an' eggs now," laughed One Leg. "People go to hell 'cause they was what they was. No one gives a cockeyed nigger for what you was. What you was is all over—has-beens ain't useful to society, nohow."

"That may be, One Leg, but a has-been's better'n a never-was, any day. What you were shows what you was—an' I was one of the two best men of his weight in the world. Think o' that, you bums and would-be yeggs! The world's damn big—and they wasn't any man in it—millions and millions o' them—that could lick me. Huh"—he looked about with scorn—"that'll make your eyes pop out like eggs—huh—the world's damn big." He raised an immense hand. "Lookit that mitt—and this mug"—putting his hand to his jaw. "It's stopped wallops from all o' them—an' the best any o' them ever got was an even break wit' me—and only one o' them ever done that.

"I used to go 'round 'em like hoops on a barrel, and they called me the Ghost wit' the Kick of a Mule. I put the fear o' Gawd in their hearts, I did. I played on their ribs till they cracked. Didden I put the Chicago Slasher out wit' a rabbit punch—and he croaks before mornin'? I'll say I been a *man* in my time!"

The derelicts looked at Husky in a disinterested manner. He rose and went on:

"When Regan was champeen, who fought him a twenty-round draw? Me! An' the gong saves him in the last round. I was gittin' better'n the twentieth. I kin hear the crowd hollerin' yit. No one ever stood up in front o' him twenty rounds before, neither. In the third round he sez to me, he sez, 'Say your prayers, Husky, you're a goin' to heaven to-night,' and I grunts back at him, 'Not till I gives you hell first,' I sez. And then we went at it. Lord Almighty, what a battle! In the 'leventh round I drops him for a count of eight. Eight, do you hear that? I just come within two counts of bein' the champeen o' the world, I did. But the Kid he gets up and shakes in his knees and then comes at me with his right sailin' plumb fer my jaw, an' quicker'n lightnin' I squared 'round'n hooked with my life—an' doubles him up like a rusty knife."

Husky gulped.

"It was a night like this an' colder'n hell wit' the door open. They was forty thousand people there, an' I come near bein' champeen. You git that—you bread beggars—you crums—you meat snatchers— you unbathed bastards! An' don't make fun o' your betters! I'm still man enough to clap your heads together." He slapped his immense broken-knuckled and finger-twisted hands together and went on: "Don't you never call me Snowbird agin, One Leg, or I'll make you pick your teeth with that crutch o' yourn. I'll make you dig your grave with it if you say I'm a hophead out loud."

One Leg looked about the room, then turned with a bored expression away from Husky. The other vagabonds did the same.

The ex-bruiser, baffled by their unconcern, trembled with the memory of past glory. The crumbling muscled hero of a little hour that had passed, he looked about forlornly.

His hands dropped from their clenched position;

his taut muscles relaxed. He jerked the soiled red kerchief from around his neck and wiped his rheumy eyes. He then seated himself by the stove. A strained silence followed.

One Leg broke it with, "Well, 'boes, any of you want to see my new invention?"

"Sure, what did you invent?" asked Weazle.

"A dog fooler," answered One Leg, pulling up the trouser of his remaining leg and showing the calf of it wrapped about with heavy brown paper. "There ain't a dog in this country can bite through that," he said proudly.

Husky felt the paper and exclaimed, "Gosh, it's only paper!"

"Sure. What did you think it was—cement?" One Leg snarled.

"Well, a fellow needs somethin' like that—there's a lot of dogs in Michigan," commented a vagabond.

"Well, I ain't very fast on this one leg," resumed the inventor, "so I had to rig up something to protect it."

"I'll bet a Newfoundlan' kin bite through that," said a vagabond who had not spoken before. "I seen 'em up in Maine bigger'n cows."

"How about a bulldog?" asked another.

"Oh, they can't bite very hard," answered One Leg. "Their jaws don't open very far. It takes a big mouth for a hard bite."

"A collie's mean, though," ventured Husky. "They'd bite their uncle if he wasn't lookin'."

"Them little terriers are pizen to me," said a nondescript. "They don't bite so hard, but they raise old Ned till they git all the darn dogs in the neighborhood after a guy."

Husky looked bored. "Let's forgit about dogs," he said. "Doc don't care about dogs, do you, Doc?"

The vagabond addressed might have been any age from fifty to eighty. His shoulders were round, his hands delicate, slender, and bloodless. His face was pinched pink and blue. His hair straggled silver into his bleared and insane eyes.

His pockets were ripped on his buttonless coat, the collar of which hid his thin neck. There remained still a touch of authority in his incisive manner, as if he belonged not in such crass surroundings. With precise enunciation he turned to his mountainous questioner.

"My name is Dr. John Abercombie, if you please, sir, and I may say that I am not at all interested in dogs—only the human brain." He raised his right hand in the manner of a professor before a class. "It is, gentlemen, the most marvelous gift of God. I speak of man's brain—not woman's."

Laughter interrupted him. He frowned at his audience.

"And I often said to her, 'But, dear, remember our position—and your own good name—even if you do not love me—you cannot afford a scandal. You surely would not trade a brain specialist for an Italian teacher of the dance! Ah, dear wife, do you not recall the words of the woman-weary Shakespeare, "Frailty, thy name is woman?" Madness lies in getting what we want—one should be careful of the brain. The convolutions of the cerebrum are many—this man belongs in the medulla oblongata position. He has touched the piamater which connects the nerves of your body —it is that most delicate portion of the brain.' "

Weazle rubbed his yellow eyebrows in a bored manner.

"Well, one thing's a cinch—none of us has any brains—that's why we're here." He looked at Doc. "Believe me, herdin' sheep in Idaho beats this life. The sheep may be dumb, but they hain't any dumber than us."

"Chortle for yourself, Weazle," snapped One Leg.

"Well, I'll sing then," returned Weazle, beginning in a cracked tenor voice:

> *"Oh, all you young Dukes and you Duchess,*
> *Just listen to what I do say,*
> *Because it ain't ourn that we touches,*
> *You send us to Botany Bay.*

"Singin' too-ral-too-ral-looralay,
And too-ral-loo-ral-lorray,
Because it ain't ourn that we touches,
You send us to Botany Bay.

"Oh had I the wings of a buzzard,
I'd spread out my pinions and fly,
'Way back to Old England forever,
And there I'd be willin' to die!"

"Gentlemen," said Doc slowly, "most anyone would be willing to die in England."

Weazle flared into a cockney accent. "England's a white man's country—and the women are all beautiful—not like in this hick country."

Doc rubbed his thin, bloodness hands and gazed at Weazle with the round eyes of the insane.

"Slandering womanhood ill becomes a gentleman, young man. Perhaps you have never known a real American woman."

"No—but that wop did."

Doc was frozen dignity.

"I shall not discuss such matters with children."

His head sank. He looked a fragment for the pity of his fellows.

All were oblivious except Husky. He rose from his seat and put a heavy hand on Doc's shoulder. "Don't take it so hard, old boy. You were up an' now you're down. I know what you mean—these yaps don't. They're just a lotta hogs an' they hain't never seen but one pen in their life. We been in real ones, ain't we, Doc?"

He patted the remnant of science. Doc did not stir.

"No use talkin' to these yaps about brains, Doc. They don't know what you mean."

The door opened.

A rugged fellow of about thirty-three entered.

It was Nitro Dugan.

He held his hands funnel-like to his mouth and blew hot breath upon them.

He wore a dark suit that had been well tailored. Full of the grease stains of the road, and pricked in several places by the sharp pieces of coke upon which he had lain, it nevertheless fit him well and accentuated the lines of his powerful body. He was over six feet tall. His hair curled around the edges of his cap. His face was intelligent and sneering; his eyes a vivid blue. He tried to smile; the sneer remained.

All in the group save Husky were deferential to the new arrival. They acted as though a man had appeared among them. He walked toward the stove.

"God Almighty, what a night! Is this all the wood you've got?" He blew on his hands again. Then, as if irritated at the scarcity of wood, "What a hell of a bunch of vagabonds and thieves you are! You'd all sit here and freeze before you'd rustle some wood."

He pushed One Leg from his chair, tore it apart, and put it in the stove.

He pulled a quart of whisky from a sagging coat pocket.

A constable's voice was heard.

"Come on, here! It's a wonder you ain't froze. You oughta be in school instead of galavantin' around the country."

He stood in the door with a youth of fine features.

All the vagabonds looked up except Doc. He still stared at the rotting floor.

The youth walked to the stove.

"They're comin' younger an' younger. Soon babies'll be on the road," laughed a vagabond.

"Yes—lovely babies," remarked Doc, looking at the youth. The sound of the constable's footsteps could be heard, dying.

Tacked to the wall was part of a map of America. Nitro Dugan walked toward it.

"It's not all here. The Gulf of Mexico and the Southern states are missing."

"Well, you don't count 'em anyhow," laughed One Leg.

Nitro traced a route with his finger.

"We're a hell of a ways from nowhere—and a long ways to go."

He walked away and stood with his back to the stove. His eyes scanned the array of derelicts.

"Where you from, Bozo?" He turned to the youth.

"Over yonder," returned the lad, circling the room with his hand.

"We're all from over yonder," put in Doc.

The wind rose in a terrifying crescendo. The kerosene lamp flickered. A shadow passed over the room.

The wind died down, then rose again, louder than before. Doors and window rattled violently.

"It'll blow the cells outta the building if it keeps this up," laughed Weazle.

"Or the wool off a sheep's tail, eh, Weaz?" suggested One Leg.

Doc spoke in a cracked, appealing voice to the youth who had taken his fancy.

"So you're from over yonder?" He broke into a half song.

> *"Over yonder, when the roll is called*
> *Over yonder—I'll be there."*

Dugan took up the words in a rich, vibrant voice.

> *"On that bright and glorious morning,*
> *When old time shall be no more,*
> *When the roll is called over yonder,*
> *I'll be there!"*

He beat time with feet and hands. The youth and Weazle took up the song.

They stopped suddenly. The wind pounded at the door. Nitro took another drink.

"Gimme a swig o' that, for God's sake!" pleaded Husky. "I'm needin' a drink for a week. I'm goin' nuts in here—two whole days of it."

"Who ran your saloon last year? I'm not feedin' good liquor to hoboes. You get a couple of swigs of this, an' it'd blow your empty can off. It's not regular liquor, you know. It's nitroglycerin. I use it for soup —it opens anything." He looked at Husky, trembling on his pine box seat.

"Lord, have a little pity, 'bo! I'd give everybody a drink if I had it. I'd give the sun away an' sit in the shade—that's why I'm here."

The man's sneer vanished for a second.

"I'll give you a swig—just to watch it work." He handed him the bottle. "Bathe your troubles on Nitro Dugan!"

The vagabonds became alert at the mention of the name.

Husky clamped his immense jaws about the neck of the bottle.

"Here—what the hell! I'm giving you a drink— not the whole bottle!"

Nitro Dugan wrestled with Husky, who held the gurgling fluid upward.

Impatient, he stepped backward and slammed a

heavy fist against Husky's jaw. The bottle broke and fell to the floor.

Husky stood, legs apart, the neck of the bottle in his mouth.

"Give a bum a horse and he'll want a stable," snapped Nitro, looking at the spilled liquor. The bottle neck rattled to the floor.

Husky's mountain of muscle trembled as though lava poured through it. He frowned at his benefactor with menace and seated himself on the pine box. Nitro sneered at him. "Now would you like some ham and eggs?" His voice rose. "What do you think I am—a traveling bartender?" Pointing to the floor—"Look what you did. You'd muss up heaven if they let you in."

Husky's heavy voice boomed, "G'wan away from me—afore I tap you on the button!"

"Don't talk to me that way, 'bo, I'll put a hole through you so big you can bury yourself in it," sneered Nitro Dugan.

"Gentlemen—gentlemen—remember where you are," pleaded Doc. "It ill behooves men to forget themselves over such trifling matters."

"Shut up!" snarled Husky, pushing the emaciated vagabond backward.

He stood before Nitro with fearful menace. "Go ahead and try to put your hole through me, 'bo.

They hain't a bullet made that kin go through my hide."

Nitro stood with his defiant sneer, his right hand buried in his coat pocket.

All eyes opened startled wide.

"Don't, for God's sake! Don't you see he's just a wreck? And now you've drove him mad with hooch," the youth pleaded.

"The hell I'm a wreck! I'm Battlin' Hagen, you whippersnapper! No long-legged sap kin talk about drillin' holes through me an' git away wit' it."

All drew in closer. The youth held Nitro's right hand. Nitro commanded, "Hands up, you bum, or I'll throw a bullet through you!"

Husky dashed toward Nitro. A bullet missed him. He twisted the snub blue revolver from Nitro's hand. The youth picked it up.

Nitro made a move for the gun, but Husky was upon him.

"Now we'll take it—man to man—you yellow dog!" Nitro, with the same defiant sneer, twisted a left fist upward. It connected under Husky's chin. The blood spurted from his teeth.

"Gentlemen, gentlemen!" pleaded Doc. A wild blow caught him. His jaw went to one side. His eyes popped. He fell unnoticed.

One Leg decided against Husky and thumped him with his crutch. The blows rattled from his head.

Then, as if irritated, Husky pulled his right shoulder back in the midst of the general mêlée. His fist caught One Leg on the right ear. It shot him perpendicular for at least six feet. He then fell like a telegraph pole, chopped low.

Husky did not look at him.

Now aroused, he rushed in relentlessly, using every trick long years in the ring had taught him.

Nitro parried, feinted, and stalled for time. His blows rattled on Husky's jaw like pebbles on an iron roof.

Hurtling bodies drowned the noise of the roaring wind. Nitro's coat was torn from his shoulders. Crushed against the door, he began to push his knees upward in an effort to cripple Husky. The ex-bruiser, equal to the occasion, used the same tactics.

"Stop it! Stop it! I'll shoot!" the youth cried.

The gun was leveled at the bloody assailants. As if eager for a breathing spell, they stopped hostilities and looked at the youth.

Doc sat erect, rubbing his jaw. He rose shakily and stood, a ghoulish spectator, blood dripping from the corners of his mouth.

One Leg still slept, like a crippled soldier, with the crutch across his breast.

The blue gun was held firmly. The monsters of men looked down its barrel.

The lamp above the youth accentuated his fine-cut features. A strand of blondish-brown hair fell from under his cap. The vagabonds faced him in a half circle as he leaned against the door.

"You wouldn't shoot, would you, kid? Why do you care if we kill each other?" coaxed Nitro.

"I don't—but if you do they'll blame it on us an' throw the key away."

"Ho, ho—that's it—lookin' out for yourself!" Nitro again sneered, stepping closer.

"Sure—ain't I human? But stand where you are!"

The revolver was shoved forward.

"Now quit your fightin'—both of you. You'll get us all thrown out in the cold. If you want a fight, beat it out of here. Then you kin freeze and go to heaven like little babies swattin' flies."

Husky sprang forward. He grabbed the gun with one hand, and with the other he ripped the youth's clothing to his waist. The lad's cap came off in the scuffle.

The half circle of vagabonds gasped in unison: "God Almighty! It's a *girl!*"

The words awoke One Leg. He clattered to his one foot.

Centuries fell from every face save Doc's. Impassive as stone, he saw not a girl, but a fellow vagabond.

The girl, with hair falling over her slender

shoulders, now stood with the expression of a trapped animal, arms folded across her breast. The half circle began to close in.

"You dirty devils! Now you want to paw me! You're all alike—every one of you—even the damned preacher in the reform school!"

Her words made them hesitate. Her left hand searched for the doorknob. An awful stillness followed. The wind could be heard trumpeting outside.

"Gentlemen, gentlemen!" pleaded Doc.

"Shut up, you nutty yap!" from Nitro Dugan.

Husky, his mind on weightier matters, held the girl's revolver in his hand. He touched the girl's arm. She shrank.

Nitro Dugan moved closer and delivered a powerful blow to Husky's jaw. He grappled for the gun.

It turned downward and exploded.

A moan followed.

The girl looked upward for a second. Her left hand searched for the doorknob again. Her right crashed the lamp to the floor. A blue flame spread over the kerosene in Husky's direction.

Dodging low, she was gone.

The door slammed shut.

Husky awaited the fast creeping flames.

Nitro Dugan jerked the door open with, "Well, it's our move—God damn the luck!"

Doc remained.

The other vagabonds scurried after Nitro Dugan. "Wait a moment, gentlemen," Doc called. "Perhaps he isn't dead."

No hobo heard.

An obscure paragraph in a Detroit paper announced next day that the jail at —— had burned to the ground.

Two unknown tramps, seeking shelter for the night, had been found dead among the ruins.

CHAPTER V
JUNGLE JUSTICE

IT WAS THE MOST MERCILESS TALE EVER TOLD IN THE jail. But no word of it was mentioned in the presence of Nitro Dugan.

All classes of wanderers were assembled in the jungle where Willow Creek joins the Mississippi River. Among them was Nitro Dugan.

Yeggs mingled freely with more common vagrants. Surrounded by their lesser satellites, they drank and made ribald laughter. Dugan was their leader.

Even with liquor roaring in their ears, the spotters for the yeggs were still furtive eyed and cautious. Spotters are the gentlemen whose sad destiny is to locate post offices in which money may be stored in iron boxes. Always they travel ahead of the box men, or yeggs. They are known in their own circle as movers (thieves on the move).

It was a festive occasion. Food was abundant. Liquor flowed freely. The social lines of hobo life had been let down. Even jungle buzzards were treated as equals. These men, who were too far down in the scale to beg or steal, and who ate the crumbs from more ambitious hoboes' tables, were now drink warmed and well fed. The word had gone out, "thumbs down for One-Lung Riley."

An ex-vagabond and criminal who had turned railroad detective, he had made a name for courage and straight shooting throughout the hobo world.

Several traps had been laid for him. He had shot his way to victory each time. An insanely brave fellow, he had learned as a lad the ways of the wandering brigades.

It was Pinkerton who said that if a man committed a crime and went on the road, finding him was like finding a needle in a haystack.

One-Lung Riley knew too much.

Defeated vengeance was now to take the form of that ironic pastime of vagabondia—the Kangaroo Court. Practiced by unlettered wanderers, it proves that irony is the last gift which society can take from the men whom it despises.

Many railroad detectives have been killed in

America. Death always meets them in the night. It generally finds them in an isolated place with no clue to the murderer.

The jungle at Willow Creek is one of the best known in America. Three miles of winding paths through a maze of undergrowth must be traversed to reach it.

For years it had been undiscovered by those disturbers of hobo peace—the railroad detectives. It had first been used as a storage place for rustlers, who boarded trains at a near-by convenient point. Before the freight had traveled many miles through the night valuable goods and the rustlers had departed from it.

So adroit were these men that all the town clowns, or local police, along the line were baffled.

The river at this point was more than a mile wide. It rolled with yellow desolation toward the Gulf of Mexico—ominous, silent, treacherous, beguiling.

Over it swept hot Southern winds and purple storms. Above it were heavy fogs and heavier clouds. The rain would roar across it in silver cycles, churning the yellow waves into white foam.

Dotted with beeches and sycamores was the neighboring state on the other shore. Strewn above with stars on clear summer nights, it was indeed a beautiful far vista for a hobo jungle.

Surrounding the jungle were scores of centuries-old live oak trees. Festooned with long streamers of Spanish moss, they resembled on misty moonlit nights the webs of mighty spiders.

The majestic river which drains ten states and parts of more than twenty others, besides two Canadian provinces—an area of land greater than ten large European countries—was at this point used by the hoboes to wash their frayed clothing.

The river was more beautiful at twilight. The surging water then took on the appearance of poured silver.

When the twilight deepened the far beeches and sycamores became blended with the softening landscape. Fireflies made magical the gathering dusk.

In the night air was the scent of crushed, damp willow trees and clover meadows wet with rain.

An old house boat was moored to some dead poplar trees at the edge of the jungle. The ropes which held the boat were worn thin from the ceaseless flow of yellow water.

A smaller jungle near the town was used to deceive the officers of the law and railroad detectives. Those vagabonds who merely stopped over in the town for a short period were content to linger at this jungle. After a hasty meal and gossip of the road they boarded the next freight train—wandering ragamuffins in a mysterious and brutal world.

For the hobo world is such that little is learned un-

less one wanders far and long. Jungles are known
from coast to coast. A straggler from Dakota who
meets one of the ragged, wandering fraternity on the
streets of a Vermont village will give him an accurate description of a railroad detective in Sacramento.
And thus the word is passed on in a world that has
no newspapers and no telephones. Happenings live in
the sordid minds of its citizens, or not at all. And only
those which reach high drama have a chance to live
until the winter snows are gone.

If a railroad detective is murdered in Butte, Montana, the news is often known in New York within a
week. Like birds which carry vermin, hoboes are ever
on the move.

But no hobo admits that he has ever been a witness
to a crime. Always has he met another vagabond who
saw another vagabond who saw the deed committed.
Hoboes are seldom naïve enough to trust their
fellows.

They brought him into the jungle at midnight.

He snarled vengeance upon all around him. He was
tall, dark, hollow cheeked, stoop shouldered. His eyebrows and mustache were red. His hair was dark. His
derby hat sat well down on his ears. His overcoat
reached to his knees and was buttoned to the throat.

The railroad detective stood before Nitro Dugan.

"Take off his bennie," commanded Nitro Dugan.

The overcoat was ripped from the detective's shoulders. It was thrown upon the ground.

"I suppose you know why you're here?" asked Nitro Dugan, looking up at the stars with unconcern.

At least two hundred vagrants stood in a circle about the two men.

There was no sound save the steady lapping of the Mississippi waves against the shore.

"No—and I don't give a damn," was the detective's answer.

Two yeggs held his arms.

"You're a tough guy, eh—you've killed eight stiffs—and only one man among 'em who could shoot straight enough to hit the side of a barn!"

The detective leaned forward, his jaw protruding. "You're a liar!"

Dugan's hand struck the man's face. It sounded like the clapping of boards together.

The man lurched forward. The yeggs gripped his arms tighter.

"Save all your strength, brother—you'll need it to push the clouds up yonder—the purple and the blue and the green ones, brother." He looked at the stars again, and then grimly at the detective. "For you're goin' to die."

"What do you mean—*die?*"

"Nothing," returned Nitro Dugan, "just *die.*" He laughed in the man's face. "It's very simple.

Everybody dies—even railroad bulls—an' the poor half-nutty bums you shot in the back—for beatin' freight trains."

"I'll see you all in jail for this! You'll pound rock for three years!" The detective was grim, defiant.

"Well, you'll never be around to see us do it—you'll be guidin' other railroad bulls to hell." Nitro Dugan's voice was iced with menace. "Can't you get next to yourself, brother, an' say your prayers? You're never goin' back home again. It's tough luck for the little wife—she'll wait breakfast for you till it's cold. You'll be a hero—dyin' in the line o' duty. The railroad'll run right along—the same old freights'll bump over the same old rails—an' all the Casey Joneses'll blow their whistles—toot toot!—straight through—an' you won't hear them never agin!" Dugan stepped closer. "We're damn good an' tired o' hearin' about you—for you're just too tough for any good reason—so that's why we're here an' you're here."

A side-wheel steamer went down the river. Its lights cut the water on each side like long, phosphorescent knives. The echo of wheel and churning water could be heard.

"We're goin' to give you a fair trial, Riley—as fair as any of us would get before any damn judge in the country. The verdict is in—but we'll go through the motions."

He turned to the assembled vagabonds.

"It's the people of the State of Poverty against One-Lung Riley. He is charged with murder—of shooting men in the backs. He is further charged with being a stool pigeon—of having been a mover who turned dick."

Dugan turned to Frisco Eddie, a shambling, apologetic spotter, who had long been known as the best paper pusher in the West. His racket had been to steal post-office money-order blanks and stamps, and then make his own money order. Liquor and other vicissitudes of easy money had at last told on his nerves. He was now nearing sixty, with hands and body that trembled like leaves falling in the river.

Frisco Eddie had never been in prison. He was one of those men who glide through life. A dipsomaniac and a dope fiend, he leaned heavily on Nitro Dugan, who had no vices save a love of life and women.

"Eddie," said Dugan, "you take charge of One-Lung's case and persecute him. You must remember as a thief with a legal diploma that if he were not guilty he would not stand here before us."

Dugan turned to Cheyenne Shorty, an ex-sheepherder, now half insane from long association with sheep. Shorty was a harmless vagabond, if sober. He was never sober. Often, at dusk, he would crawl on his hands and knees and bleat at the sky like a sheep.

"Shorty, you defend One-Lung. You're about the

type of lawyer a tramp would get in another court."

"Thank you," smiled Cheyenne.

"We will now open the court with prayer. Frisco Eddie, lead off. Bow your crummy heads, brothers."

Frisco Eddie's cracked voice began:

"O Lord, Our Heavenly Father of the first well-known hobo, Jesus, look down upon us who are about to commend an immortal soul to Thy great care! Thou great befriender of working girls, who showest them the way to spend their six dollars a week wisely, and to resist the temptations of the flesh, we ask Thee for divine guidance for what we are about to do.

"If we unduly throw this soul in Your face, Lord, it is because we do not know what in hell to do with it. We realize, dear Lord of us all, Your position in this most trying moment. Neither would we, as humble vagrants along the eternal shore, be guilty of sending one to You whom You could not easily make use of. A stool pigeon of the first order, Lord, he would keep holy the dark places of heaven and bring before Your divine officers the indiscretions of Your most beautiful angels. For beauty has ever been tempted, dear Lord, on earth as it is in heaven.

"Lucifer, the proud, in all his glory will not be arrayed in more of Thine eternal salvation than One-Lung. It is true that there may be those who go to Thy everlasting arms of resting and need no mourners here below. Rather they should be joyful and sing hosannas in Thy great name.

"A brand snatched from the burning, Lord—a poor soul in Thy blessed image made weary from shooting his own kind. You have ever been on the side of the downtrodden, Lord. You make the spuds to grow near the jungle and the chicken to wander free from care into our willing hands. You help us in the gathering of food for our slumgullions. You allow us to wander on the open road and give us the blessed benediction of heaven.

"For is it not true, dear Lord—

> *"That beggars who walk,*
> *And queens who ride*
> *To the Valley of Skulls,*
> *Sleep side by side?*

"It is a beautiful night, Lord, upon which to die. The stars and the moon and the beautiful river shall sing his threnody. And, Lord, if one of us should be shuffled off the gallows to dance with broken arches before Thy throne, it would not be amid such beauty. Rather would the knot be tied behind our left ears, Lord, and as we fell through the trap, dear Lord, the knot would jerk our heads forward and break our immortal necks, dear Lord. We would hang like a cracked scarecrow, All-merciful Lord, while a doctor listened to our hearts pounding their way on the road to Your blessed arms, dear Lord.

"But, Blessed Lord, we are not as those men who do such deeds. We profess no creed, dear Lord. We are but humble servants in Thy name. Ours is a gentler method, Lord. It comes suddenly, Lord. The soul of the departed flies suddenly before You from a hole which a bullet makes. It is more lenient, Lord. There is dignity in death by a bullet. . . ."

"Shut up!" snapped Dugan. "Do you think you're the only one He's got to listen to?"

Frisco Eddie resumed: "For they who taketh up the Smith and Wesson must die by a Colt, for so it is written, ever and anon, before dinner and after, from now on, Amen."

Weak, bearded, and grimy chins were lifted. Bodies moved. Feet scraped over the hard ground. A drunken derelict yelled:

> *"Amen—Hobo Ben,*
> *Chased a pig an' caught a hen!"*

"Choke that crummy noose dodger, someone," commanded Nitro Dugan.

A scuffle followed. A body fell.

Frisco Eddie chanted dolefully:

> *"It matters not, so I've been told*
> *Where the body lies when the heart is cold."*

"Come on, let's start the trial," cut in Dugan. He smiled urbanely at the detective and asked, "What have you to say before sentence is passed upon you?"

"Sentence? Good God, you're a gang of yeggs! Who the hell are you to try an officer of the law? You can't do it. Even if you were honest men. I haven't been tried yet."

"Your disrespectful dishonor to your God, your country, and your wife—I object to the prisoner's vile language. It is only fit to be used in a group of private detectives. He takes the name of Almighty God in vain—for it'll do him no good here . . ."

Frisco Eddie raised a trembling right hand. There was laughter.

"Keep your traps shut, everybody in the court-room," said Dugan. He looked about him. "We can't open court without a picture of George Washington and a flag that needs washing, and, besides—there's not a Bible here. Bring us a book, somebody."

A vagrant stepped forward with a dime novel.

"Stand there and hold it." Turning to the assem-blage—"Swear to commit perjury on that book. One book's as good as another to all dishonest men. Now, prisoner, what was your last remark?"

The detective answered with a sneer, "I said I hadn't been tried yet."

"Oh, well, that's a small matter. That's what the thieves of the law call Jewish prudence. We'll pass sentence on you and then try you—all the leading newspapers do that now."

Levity deserted Dugan's voice. Clouds slid over the moon. A musty, river-laden breeze swept across the jungle.

"You are to be shot through the heart, Riley—at an unexpected moment."

Bleared faces became serious. Dugan resumed. "The court is in session—call the witness for the persecution."

"Your Honor," Frisco Eddie began blandly, addressing Nitro Dugan, "as this is a matter of life and death we must make haste. As you have placed upon my tired legal shoulders the responsibility of this man's future, and as the witnesses are so numerous against him, I have decided to call but two men in order that Justice may not be blinded by too many facts."

He cleared his withered and bony throat.

"I will first call Ypsilanti Slim. When you have heard enough of his testimony I will then call my next witness. Ypsilanti Slim, step forward."

No more terrible specimen than Ypsilanti Slim walked under the moon that night. He resembled an ogre that had been torn full grown and insane from the womb of time. Nurtured in violence, his eyes were hyena-like. A leering slacker in the eternal economic masquerade, he required only the make-up that God and his mother had given him. Even vaga-bonds, long schooled in horror, looked at him intently.

His complexion was yellow and green. His eyes were crossed. One was smaller than the other. He was short and pot-bellied. His legs curved in at the knees and were wrapped about with pieces of filthy rag carpet. His feet were large and flat. He was coatless. His black satine shirt was streaked white from the dried perspiration of many weeks. His trousers were held with three old pieces of suspender tied about the waist. His body was sunk in the middle as though it were too much effort to hold it erect.

His nose was long, bulbous, purple, and pimply red. His lower lip hung loose, swollen, cracked.

One-Lung Riley stood like a dazed spectator, not believing his eyes.

"Your Honor," smiled Frisco Eddie, "this is Ypsilanti Slim. His moniker may not sound right, but he'd be slim if he stood up straight."

Dugan, now murder bent, paid no attention.

"Do you know One-Lung Riley?" he asked the life-twisted witness.

"I do," returned Ypsilanti Slim, his eyes looking in several directions. "I first went on the road wit' him. We kicked in a car in Cheyenne, and Jeff Carr, the big dick there, got us. One-Lung here squealed, an' I got the works for two years—poundin' rocks wit' a sledge."

The witness glowered at the detective, who returned his glance with scorn.

Ypsilanti Slim continued: "When he turned rat on me I makes up my mind I'd git even—but I don't need to do that—his record here's enough. Hain't he been promoted till he's the Chief Bull on a thousand miles o' track? Diden' they find the Duke o' York wit' a bullet in his dome? It was in all the papers—I got some pieces here." He pulled three oilcloth-wrapped yellow pieces of newspaper from his hip pocket and read, " 'Brave officer o' the law,' it says here, 'routs three desprit criminals—kills one.' "

The expression on Nitro Dugan's face did not change. The English bandit whose moniker was the Duke o' York had been a loyal friend in his bullet-ridden life.

"Call the next witness," said Nitro Dugan.

Frisco Eddie called a youth of less than twenty.

"Do you know this man?"

"Yes, sir, I seen him. One-Lung Riley, the dick."

"What's your charge against him?"

"He shot my buddy in the back. I drug him outta the yards till I got him to the hospital. The doctors slipped him the 'black bottle'—and he died."

A deep lull, then quick movement followed the words. The black bottle had been mentioned. It is the firm belief among hoboes that destitute men are given poison from a black bottle to rid the earth of their presence.

"How do you know it was the black bottle?" asked Dugan.

"Because there was stains on his cheeks—they run down the corners of his mouth—that's how."

Every face turned toward One-Lung Riley.

He stood defiant, seeming much taller under the downward moon.

"It's a damn lie. The kid shot at me, and I shot back."

"Shut up!" commanded Dugan.

"I didn't know they slipped 'em the black bottle up this way," said a voice from the gathering.

The trial was halted a moment.

Cheyenne Shorty replied, "Sure they do—it's always at midnight—you're poundin' your ear restin' easy like wit' your mouth open—then they come in soft—pet you a little an' fix the covers—an' slip you the bottle. Just a touch of it is all you need. It burns your heart right out."

The jungle became alert. One-Lung Riley watched with apprehension. There followed the hum of many voices.

Frisco Eddie, trembling more than usual, addressed the young hobo, who also trembled.

"Where was your buddy from?"

"Up in Alaska somewhere. I met him in Seattle a

year ago. We was pals ever since. He'd give you his shirt—afore they slipped him the black bottle."

Nitro Dugan looked sternly at One-Lung Riley. He read the startled expression and then asked the youth with deadly wisdom, "Did he have any folks?"

Dugan waited for the effect of the words on the crowd.

"Yes, sir, his mother, but I won't tell her. She won't wait for him if she knows he's dead. For he says to me, he says, one time when we were beatin' it down in Florida—you know it's tough down there—well, he says, 'If I ever git bumped off, don't you tell no one anything about me' . . . an' I promised I wouldn't."

"That's enough," said Dugan, glancing at a few clouds. "It looks like rain."

There was a hurried consultation. Nitro Dugan, Frisco Eddie, Cheyenne Shorty were surrounded. Nearly all moved to the rear of One-Lung Riley.

The terrible gathering pressed more closely toward the doomed detective. His eyes roved over the few hard, moon-clouded faces in front of him. There could be heard the ripple of water and the rattling of leaves in the wind.

And then, for the first time, a look of terror came into his eyes. It was as if he saw ghouls opening the gates of eternity.

"Holy God in heaven, men—you wouldn't do this!"

"The hell we wouldn't," flared back Nitro Dugan. "You're just crazy if you think we wouldn't."

"Yes, indeed, One-Lung," chimed in Frisco Eddie, rubbing thin and bloodless hands, "he who lives by murder must die by murder. We didn't make the law— it is eternal—we merely enforce it."

Deeply apologetic, he stood before the man who was about to die. Again his cracked voice chanted:

> *"It matters not, so I've been told,*
> *Where the body lies when the heart is cold."*

Nitro Dugan turned sternly.

"Shut up with that God-damned song! Is that all you know? What the hell's that got to do with this?"

He turned to One-Lung Riley, who stood with pride abandoned. His lower lip hung loosely. His teeth chattered twice. "Be game, Riley—be game—you're Irish, you know—just like me. There's nothing crueler than an Irish cop—so take it standing up and consider yourself damn' lucky you don't get worse. For two cents I'd have you stood up against a tree and have this gang bang the buttons off your vest with bullets. What about the kid whose fingers you smashed when he tried to get on a freight? You came down the ladder and smashed 'em—and he had to have 'em cut off. But to hell with all that! You plinged the Duke o' York—can't you hear him laughin' up in the trees?

You got him by accident—he was probably full of hop. And you want to watch . . . he'll knock the hell out of your soul before it reaches God—it's a million miles up there, you know."

The detective's mouth opened as if to plead.

"Tell it to God," snarled Nitro Dugan.

The detective's face was a mask of agony. He tried to hold his hands together. The yeggs held him tighter. Two jungle buzzards approached Dugan.

"It's all ready."

"We won't need it—buryin's too good for him— let him feed the carp in the river."

"Please, please . . . my wife!"

Frisco Eddie buried a trembling chin in his breast. He closed wet eyes.

Dugan nudged him in the ribs. "Come out of it, you fool—he wouldn't cry for *you!*"

"I wasn't crying—for Christ's sake!"

Gael looked at Gael.

"Good-bye, Riley"—from Nitro Dugan. Then to the brigands in the rear, "Hey, fellows." Those in front stepped aside.

A spurt of blue flame followed.

The detective's eyes opened wide. His chin fell. He plunged forward, swimmerlike, and lay still.

"Bring on a log here, you fellows—quick."

A group of vagabonds hurried forward with a log. Knives flashed. The body was stripped, mutilated.

"Bury the clothes"—to the buzzards.

The pockets were turned inside out.

The nude body was tied to the log and carried to the river by many vagabonds. Others gathered around them.

Dugan led the way.

"Now all together."

Caught by the current, the log turned three times, the body underneath.

The moon slanted its rays across the mighty yellow river.

The vagabonds watched, silent, as if a ship were gliding out of the harbor.

"Now, don't bunch up in the yards! Scatter to get your trains," commanded Dugan as he left with Frisco Eddie.

The many paths along the river were soon dark with gliding outcasts and brigands.

In a short time the jungle was silent.

CHAPTER VI
A SPRIG OF WHITE LILAC

Two mexicans entered the prison accused of rape by a free-for-all young lady.

When her character became known to the judge he sentenced them to thirty days for disturbing the peace.

They did not smile once during their entire sentence.

With the Mexicans came an epidemic of crabs. They are a species of insects which bury their heads in the body. The prisoners used blue ointment to kill them.

The ointment contained mercury. A convict who had studied pharmacy used it to shine pennies. He made the copper turn to the color of silver.

Always, if placed with a nickel, which was larger,

the penny would pass for a dime among the unwary.

The guards brought things to the inmates—for a price. One green guard was mortified to discover that he owned thirty-three pennies which he thought were dimes.

The day upon which we bathed was sometimes suddenly changed without notice. It would give the guards a chance to search the cells if we were unexpectedly marched to the bath. The herders of men often purloined things which they had themselves smuggled into the jail.

Every seven days we were allowed to bathe. And once it was fourteen days. Eddie Evans had an effeminate love of luxury, which I, the son of Irish peasants, did not find displeasing. After the eighth day Eddie became irritable and had the audacity to ask a guard if he could not take a bath.

The herder of men moved a quid of tobacco from one cheek to another. He smeared the iron floor with fluid. Then he laughed grimly. "Who do you think you are—a guard?"

"Do guards bathe?" Eddie asked innocently.

The prisoners jeered.

The guard turned quickly.

Before long Eddie was put in "the hole"—solitary confinement for forty-eight hours.

The mania for cigarettes permeated the jail. When

too short to be held with the fingers they were placed on toothpicks or the sharp ends of burnt matches, that one more puff might be obtained from them

Eddie begged for a cigarette. The guard gave some to him. But he gave no match.

The boy kept the cigarettes some hours. Finally the guard came and gave him some matches. But he first took the cigarettes.

To his consternation he found one cigarette was missing from the pack. He returned to the hole and found Eddie smoking nonchalantly.

He was given another twenty-four hours.

Eddie had some talent as an engraver. He would copy with lead pencil crude pictures from cheap magazines with accurate detail.

He often expressed a desire to manufacture money in competition with the government. He wanted me to embark in the same business with him.

"All you'll have to do is pass the money," he assured me. From a mixture of fear and patriotism, I refrained.

Never was it more aptly proven that necessity is the mother of invention than in the jail.

We would wash our linen and place it wet against the hot iron wall. It would adhere closely, even when dry. We would remove it, as smooth as if it had been ironed.

We were once given bread pudding which we could not eat. The sauce was made of some concoction never before seen in the world.

A full-page picture of the governor of the state was in the Sunday supplement of the newspaper. We pasted his hard features to the wall with the sauce.

A Republican guard looked at the picture and admired our zeal. A Democrat guard who talked with an Irish brogue made us remove the picture.

So well did the sauce act as glue that paint and small flakes of iron were removed with the picture.

A group of women were imprisoned for light offenses in a building adjacent. We could only see the tops of their heads as they moved by the window. Even that was a pleasure. Often we speculated on whether or not they were beautiful.

The floor above us jailed the girls accused of more serious offenses. Often we could talk to them through the ventilator.

Dates were made in this manner if the going-out period coincided.

It was said in the jail that once a rapist made a date with a murderess. They escaped from the jail, and in three months a baby boy was born. He looked like the head guard.

He became a well-known lawyer and later was elected governor. Brother Jonathon always adorned the tale with a moral. "Young men can go far if their parents can only escape from jail in time," he would say.

Communication via the ventilator was strictly forbidden. The rule was as strictly disregarded.

A jailbird whose sentence was about to expire made an engagement with an unseen lady with a lovely voice. She lulled him to distraction. He was to meet her the evening of his release. She, too, had been unjustly detained. They would begin life anew.

An hour before his expected release he was told that he must remain in jail a month longer. The charming lady with whom he had made the engagement was the matron.

He remained, dejected, among us; his faith in women forever gone.

Women with nasal voices and.sad faces wandered in and out of the jail each Sunday.

With different beliefs they fought the battle of God for the conquest of our souls.

One wore upon her ample bosom a sprig of white lilac. Up and down it moved as on a billow of ocean as she sang. Never was anything more beautiful in an iron world without flowers. The slender pear-shaped blossoms and the delicately traced leaves were in lovely contrast upon her mercerized black silk jacket.

A triumvirate of devotion, Eddie Evans, Blink, and I, watched the lilac carefully.

Finally the lady became warm with singing and expostulation. She removed the short black coat.

She left without the lilac.

Blink divided it in three pieces.

CHAPTER VII
THE GIVER OF LIFE

Like most smart men, brother Jonathon was only in jail by accident. He might have been released on bail. Under the circumstances, that procedure did not appeal to him. He considered his arrest an affront to his personal dignity. By some stubborn quirk of the brain, he felt that by remaining in jail he would shame the officials of the law.

"I am being persecuted for diversion," he often said. "The diversion of fools who would imprison their superiors."

He knew the names of the swinging constellations.

He often told fortunes with the aid of astrology. It relieved him at times of the monotony of medicine selling.

Rustics gazed wide eyed as he spoke flippantly of

Aquarius, Orion, and Telescopium. Pointing heavenward he would shout: "There is no room for petty vanity in the hearts of men who study the stars."

While allowing a rustic to gaze through a telescope for a modest fee he had been arrested. The charge against him was that of operating a public business without a licence. The police tried to prove that Brother Jonathon had confederates who were ungentlemanly enough to pick the honest farmer's pockets while he gazed at the starry heavens.

Brother Jonathon was indignant at the charge. "A gentleman and a scholar, a man of medicine and abstruse science, taken down the street as though he were a common thief—with a thief of the law on each side of him. I shall take the case to the Supreme Court of Washington. I have the distinguished honor of knowing Chief Justice White. We each served in the gallant cause of the Confederacy, and he shall not allow a comrade in arms to languish in a common jail."

He was a superior individual who had shaken dice with life.

The old man was without a peer in conducting a patent medicine show. That he should expostulate in a jail with ordinary rascals was a tax to his sense of humor. He smiled readily, except when his attorney, or his wife, called. That was always an occasion for the abuse of lawyers and women in general.

Brother Jonathon was the shrewdest man in the

carnival world. He sent funds by registered mail to his bank every week. Penurious and profligate, he would haggle over a dime—and take the loss of ten thousand dollars with a smile and a platitude.

His hair had once been red. That was long ago. It was now a dismal yellow-gray. But his eyebrows were still red. They overhung kindly, furtive, sad, and mocking eyes.

They were pantherlike eyes in which defiance lurked behind somnolent surrender.

His real name was supposed to be Jonathon Maloney. But he preferred to be called Brother Jonathon.

He always wore an immense hat, a dark well-tailored suit, and a long drooping mustache. His gloves and spats were of the same color as his suit. He was never without a large, gold-headed ebony walking stick. Engraved upon the gold were the words:

To the Giver of Life
from
The Children of Chicago.

He spoke in a deep, powerful, well-modulated voice. His English, in public, was nearly correct and always precise.

An unabridged dictionary, a morocco-bound copy of some materia medica, a red volume on anatomy, the complete works of Shakespeare, a worn edition of Rabelais, and an expensive Bible made up his traveling library.

He called all his books Bibles—and read them constantly.

He impressed me greatly at the time. And ever since he has had a chosen niche in the crowded hall of my memory. Indeed it would not surprise him to know of the place he occupies in *Jarnegan* and in the present volume.

"If you'll keep out of jail long enough, my boy," he used to say, "you may write a book that men will read. But may the great and glorious and all-loving God preserve me from such a task."

I was later to be a helper in Brother Jonathon's medicine show.

In wintry or summer weather, on mud or pavement, he would walk for an hour or two each night—alone.

In common with all mankind, he carried his half truths seriously.

He knew the Old Testament well. He spoke of the ancient prophets as though they were his personal friends.

He called Shakespeare "William," and spoke of his characters as though they were members of his patent medicine show. His favorite was Falstaff.

Rabelais was always "Rab" to him. "It means mad

—rabid. He was Falstaff's brother. They were both drunkards—like William."

Whenever he heard a strange word he looked it up in his dictionary.

He talked glibly of the great of the earth. They, like the prophets, were his personal friends.

John L. Sullivan and Grover Cleveland were his favorites. He would astonish people in small towns by saying, "I told John not to fight Corbett when he did." Then, sighing, "It was the one time he wouldn't listen to me."

A country editor was often greeted with: "Grover told me that being President was about like running a newspaper—one had to keep a lot of damn fools in line. I don't think any man ever appreciated the American newspaper and its diversified functions like Grover. I'll never forget the time he fell in the water at Buzzards Bay. Joe Jefferson and I pulled him out. A great man, Grover!"

Brother Jonathon claimed to be of the landed gentry in Ireland. He was a magnificent liar. If he happened to be talking to an Englishman he would say: "Yes, yes, we have a lot in common—my mother was English—she married my father when he was on a vacation from Trinity College. The Maloneys, you know, were long pillars of the state in Ireland. Edmund Burke relied a great deal on the Maloneys."

If the new acquaintance were a Frenchman:

"Marvelous people, the French—my mother was from Tours—I owe all my success to my French sense of humor. What was it Voltaire said: 'If there were no French, God would have to invent some'?"

When introduced he would always say, "Call me Brother Jonathon." Then, with reverence, "The Giver of Life."

He was the world's great democrat. He claimed admixture with all the races of the earth. Oriental, Judean, Ethiopian—all had some connection with him—in his conversation.

He was a genius in diplomacy. His gifts were such that he could dominate any gathering with his poise, tact, and personality.

He made use of all these qualities in being a patent medicine faker.

At times one felt that his mind was full of cant. Diplomat and hypocrite, he seemed to believe in his nostrums. There were other times when one was not so sure. "Poverty is the mother of crime," he would often say, and add: "Necessity knows no law. It makes cowards of us all—for we are such stuff as dreams are made of, and our turbulent lives are rounded with a sleep—one should study the stars to gain equilibrium.

"Alas, poor Shakespeare—red-haired drunkard whose ocean of a brain touched all the shores of thought." His eyes would narrow. "I wonder what he thought of his daughters who could not read, and of the boy he wrote the sonnets to. He was quite a person was William—one of my own kind of people— he makes me doubt the possibility of death. Surely that brain is not the dust of English worms now. Surely a God would form itself out of nothing to protest against such a crime.

"Fifty years was not long enough for such a mind and soul—perhaps they live again in me—I have all the moods of that mighty man. As I say, William makes me doubt the possibility of death. . . ."

He was all things to all men—and more than that to women. But no priest was ever as dogmatic as Brother Jonathon in his belief that in the purity of women was the salvation of the world. As in all great hypocrites, there was in him the muddle of the fanatic.

As he conversed with one, into his panther-like eyes would creep contempt, as though he had correctly measured everything.

Brother Jonathon's mind and heart were never at peace.

He would glance at the audience and confide: "They want something for nothing—the poor fools—their greed might possibly be assuaged—their stupidity can only be cured by death."

After hearing of how two yokels had fought over a girl's good name, as it was known in that section, he commented: "Every blow struck in defense of a woman's honor is a blow struck against her."

He would talk instantly and grandiloquently of flowers, women, bees, or birds.

Before an audience, he would suddenly launch into any subject that struck his fancy, or that had recently come into his mind.

"Ah, my friends," would come the heavily crooned words, "there are mysteries as unfathomable as loved women's hearts. For instance," he would ask startlingly, "why does a mocking bird return to the same tree year after year? Why do they sing only at night? These are among the many unanswered questions of the ages, my friends.

"Silent all day, my friends, as gray and meek as doves, they awake like burglars after midnight and pour stolen music on the world. And they all have different melodies and different tunes. They sing not like one another—and no sound that any of them makes is their own. Individualists supreme, with larceny in their souls, they steal the gurgling sonnets of the glorious lark of the meadow and the throaty notes of the golden thrush. They borrow the raucous cries of the sea gulls and the shrill notes of the peaceful quail. They rob the blackbirds of their chirps and the sparrows of their twittering. They warble like roller canaries and quarrel like woodpeckers over a worm. They sing until dawn—and then their hearts become as still as a little child in its mother's arms after a careful dose of Giver of Life."

Sometimes Brother Jonathon would walk upon the platform with inebriated dignity under control. He would smack his lips and begin:

"Fellow citizens, patriots, in the common cause of diversified humanity, the birds of the air have even a greater contemporary in the rôle of animalism and profound mystery. I speak of the dog. During my early sojourn as a medicine vendor to the King of China, I noted that great monarch's affection for a type of dog which is the national pet. It is known as a chow. It was as yellow as a lawyer's liver. They are vicious to all and sundry for the first few years until, as it were, they get to know you. Then, after many bites and bruises inflicted more or less cruelly, they become affectionate. The King could never understand the great heart, the magnificent understanding of this breed of dog, which started rightly in the King's opinion by hating mankind and ended up in loving it. It told the King more than all the writings of Confucius. That dabbler in schoolboy wisdom began by loving mankind. The chow was born into the world with hatred. Centuries of treacheries, murders, deceits, strangulations, all evils, had accumulated in a ball of ether and had been swallowed by the dog's ancestors.

"Three of these dogs, now gentle as kittens, were my snarling companions when I invented my first bottle of Giver of Life.

"On rainy days in the far interior of that heathen country I would give them each a spoonful of the medicine divine. It brought out their doghood and not even a mandarin could touch them.

"The King saw with dazed eyes the grand transformation in the national dog. He made Giver of Life the medicine plenipotentiary to the bedroom of the King.

"It soothed maidens and made confessions more easy on their wedding nights.

"The King ordered five thousand bottles each week for his harem.

"The medicine grew so popular in China that maidens cried for it, instead of their husbands or other men. The King then with great and royal reluctance ordered that under pain of death it be forbidden women *under eighty*."

Brother Jonathon made a dramatic pause. He was, at such times, a man born with the lightning. His tall and majestic frame quivered with intense fervor. He had the art of the mountebank; he believed for the moment that which seethed in his brain.

"The wisdom of earth is not as important as the ring in a bull's nose," he often said when drunk. He treated it accordingly.

"But ah, gentlemen and ladies, a strange thing happened when the women of eighty were the sole partakers of Giver of Life." He would smile broadly. "But I can only tell that to you men. . . ."

Brother Jonathon was fond of cats. They made their way to him in every town.

"They're the greatest creatures in the world—they never let down the bars."

Among his close friends he was not so careful of his English. His argot was of underworld Europe, Australia, and America.

He called police informers narks, as they do in the London slums. His wife was always Storm and Strife —possibly from Australia. Men released from prison were sprung, and when he wrote a letter he always flew a kite.

So accomplished was he as a circus and carnival linguist that he often conversed for hours in that idiom without the use of a straight English phrase.

Brother Jonathon's wife was gray and worn. She wore a black jet bonnet. She alternated two dresses— both buttoned tightly down the front. One was lavender, the other black. Her blunt, nail-bitten fingers projected red and white from black, half-fingered gloves. She was quiet, unassuming, self-effacing and self-sacrificing.

Liquor was a passion with Brother Jonathon. He passed long hours in saloons.

He preferred to drink beer directly out of the bottle. It was his method to allow all the bottles to stand on the bar when empty. He would pay the final score by counting them. When the bill came to an uneven sum he would toss slightly under the amount on the bar and say, "I guess that's near enough." His effrontery usually startled the bartender into silence.

If others in his party drank anything besides beer he would have the bartender keep the amount on a tab. He would then argue over the sum until the bartender was in confusion. But instead of that gentleman being angry he would more often be apologetic. Brother Jonathon would smile in a fatherly way and explain gently: "That's all right, my boy—we all make mistakes. The big men always admit them. In that way lies growth."

Umbrellas often hung carelessly on the bar. Brother Jonathon absent-mindedly walked away with more than twoscore during one rainy week. If detected he would become elaborately apologetic. His sincerity was never doubted. Often the owner would treat Brother Jonathon to a drink.

He used the umbrellas to good advantage. Bartenders, fair-ground managers, baggage agents, and hotel proprietors received them as gifts.

He would say, "Make things pay for things—we live in a trading age." Then with a chuckle, "It's all in the spirit of fun."

Brother Jonathon always advertised in the New York *Clipper*, "the showman's Bible." His advertisement was worded:

BROTHER JONATHON wants swell dressers on and off. Versatile performers, song and dance people, magician, sister team, hoop roller, ventriloquist. No boozers or chasers. No tickets unless I know you. I pay railroad fare after joining. Tourists save stamps. Ventriloquist must double in Punch. First part and afterpiece. Also a B.F. [blackface] comedian. Three Card Monte please write. All performers double on canvas.

Rehearsal consisted of sitting around in a circle and running through the lines. Nothing was ever written. The carnival vagabonds knew their work by heart.

In conversation he was grandiose and benevolent toward his employees. In reality he was a ruthless autocrat.

His phobia was against what he called chasers—men in his company who sought the society of women in the towns they visited. They were strictly forbidden to do so. He levied fines against them constantly.

From his judgment there was no appeal. The legality of his fines was never questioned. He would often take back half of a carnival vagabond's weekly salary.

Brother Jonathon had a big medicine show. The smaller shows had but one or two singers. They worked on an open lot or a side street.

Brother Jonathon charged ten cents for standing room and twenty-five cents for seats.

The tourists mentioned in his advertisement were performers who would send for tickets if they wished to travel in that direction and then leave the train before reaching the show, thus making railroad fare. Brother Jonathon always considered the show a necessary evil to attract the crowd. His whole aim was to sell his medicine, Giver of Life. It was a "spiritual, mental, and physical cure-all."

He had once sold the formula of a concoction to a firm of patent-medicine manufacturers for ten thousand dollars. He bought worthless gold stock with the money. But when he talked of the transaction:

"Yes, yes, I own fifty-two per cent. of the stock in Allevan's gold mine out in Death Crossing, Nevada. We have three hundred men operating there now—most satisfied miners you ever beheld—a thriving community. I was there last Christmas and gave each family a bottle of Brother Jonathon's Giver of Life. Strange to say, those seeds planted out of kindness have sprouted many oaks in that desert country, as it were. They keep sending and sending for the Life Giver."

Brother Jonathon carried a broken-down physician

with him during the summer. A weak weed of humanity, this physician lingered on year after year. Brother Jonathon picked him up in April and dropped him each November.

"Doctor Fitzmaurice will never die—he's soaked in alcohol," was the medicine faker's estimate.

All that was really left of the doctor was his diploma from a great medical college. It was by flaunting this medical shell that Brother Jonathon kept from the clutches of the law.

The doctor seldom talked. He was never without his bottle and was never in the foreground. He was known as Brother Jonathon's secretary.

Dr. Fitzmaurice spoke of Brother Jonathon as "the Doctor." Little worms of mockery crawled around the words. It was the way in which he showed contempt. He had once called him "A Napoleon of fakers."

Brother Jonathon returned with a twisted smile: "You flatter Napoleon. He never knew when to laugh —*I do.*"

That night he gave Dr. Fitzmaurice two quarts of old Kentucky Bourbon.

Brother Jonathon loved all that pertained to medicine. Once, after a long walk under the stars, he returned to Dr. Fitzmaurice with the words, "Doctor, I think you have thrown a world away."

Dr. Fitzmaurice, with an empty bottle and a shaking hand, retorted, "No, Doctor, the world has thrown me away—just like an empty bottle of Giver of Life."

He rubbed his bottle with thin fingers and addressed Brother Jonathon: "What fools these mortals be! Eh, *Doctor?* Perhaps *you* are wasting *your* life."

Brother Jonathon caught the scorn in the words but ignored it. Then, smiling:

> *"Then they for sudden joy did weep,*
> *And I for sorrow sung*
> *That such a King should play Bo-Peep,*
> *And go the fools among."*

He looked kindly at Dr. Fitzmaurice and the empty bottle and continued:

"Yes, yes, Doctor—perhaps we are both wasting our lives. Shakespeare knew the tragedy of genius: 'It must go the fools among!'"

Brother Jonathon always sent patients to Dr. Fitzmaurice. The doctor prescribed the Giver of Life for all ailments, including brain fever and the longing after immortality.

Brother Jonathon did not mingle with the crowd. Upon entering a strange town he would walk with precise dignity down the main street, his gold-headed cane tapping the sidewalk.

He would introduce himself to the postmaster, the mayor, and the leading tradesmen. His list of small purchases was the same in each town. His engaging personality made him known.

Never did he fail to placate the local doctors. He swam in a sea of medical inferences before them. If he did not gain their respect he at least made them submit to his personality.

He had one sure way to win them. He would become ill and call in several of them for a conference over his condition. This method never failed. "In spite of my own years of medical research I still have faith in my fellow physicians." This would appear in the local papers.

A vaudeville act and the afterpiece followed his medicine talk. Brother Jonathon had discovered this method to be safe. In his early career many people had walked out on his medical oration when it was the last thing on the program.

He mixed his medicine in a large wooden tub. He wore rubber gloves and a physician's white linen coat which reached to his knees. He tied a towel around his head, the ends of which hung down his back.

There was a benignly happy expression on his face as he poured the liquid into scores of bottles. His wife washed and labeled the bottles. She allowed no one to talk to Brother Jonathon while he was at work.

His formula contained three fourths water. The rest was Epsom salts, powdered rhubarb, licorice powder, burnt sugar, and wintergreen essence.

"Water is a great healer—three fourths of the earth's surface is water," he often remarked.

The performers could stay at a hotel if they paid their own way. Otherwise they slept in the medicine tent.

If business was bad Brother Jonathon would arrange for a grand drawing with a local furniture dealer. A complete bedroom or dining-room set would be offered as a prize to the person drawing the lucky ticket with a bottle of medicine. The drawings would take place after all the medicine possible had been sold.

A vast crowd attended the grand drawing. The furniture would be in view in a prominent store window for days. Far in advance Brother Jonathon would arrange with a local person to "win" the prize. It was then turned back to the dealer, who profited by the advertising.

The lucky local person was given six bottles of the Giver of Life.

Just before leaving town Brother Jonathon would arrange with the local drug stores to take many bottles of his product at half price.

The ingredients mixed, the show would begin. The band blared. Song, dance, minstrel jokes, all manner of crude humor and sentimentality followed. Before the grand climax Brother Jonathon would step upon the stage. He would time the suspense with which he was awaited. Scanning the audience carefully, he would talk in a confidential manner and cause loud laughter by giving a humorous narrative in which lonesome Ed Farley figured.

After the audience was through laughing over Farley's exploit he would tell how he once saved Farley's life with Giver of Life.

Taking a bottle from his assistant he would say, "Dear, faithful Giver of Life—the never failing!"

Standing dramatically erect, his chest thrown back, his right hand laid flat across his heart, he would look longingly at the bottle and then at his performers.

A few slight coughs, and his hand would come slowly from his heart and be raised in air.

"Of course, lad-ees and gentlemen, you realize by now that my entire fortune and my whole soul is wrapped up in this blessed medicine. To improve the health of humanity is my unerring motive. And in so doing I have gathered together this incomparable band of musicians of the first grade."

The musicians would bow.

"They are a high salaried group of people who have played before kings and society women the world over, as far as the land of the Zulus and

Europe. It would interest you each and all to know that Sousa, the great band leader, once played with my troupe in the early days. There is no such music as we give you—and all—to heal the sick—to keep comfort from the dying by robbing death of its terrors—and assuaging the grief stricken and the lowly."

He held the bottle high above his head.

"It is not for profit that medicine is sold by me. In proof of this astonishing and altruistic fact I offer you this living, final, and definite proof."

The left forefinger touched the lower portion of the bottle.

"You will note that the price is here plainly marked that all who runs may read—two dollars—two dollars—lad-ees and gentlemen—two dollars. By the ethics of medicine and mutual agreements of treaties and codicils between states and nations no man is allowed to mark such a price on a bottle of health-giving fluid unless by agreement of the world's leading chemists and anthropologists, zoölogists, and pedastical somnambulists, which includes the various clergy and men of all creeds, unless—excuse my digression—that man has proven that which he sells is worth double the price, he cannot sell it, or mark it, even at that price. For, as you know, men of medical jurisprudence are men who believe and love humanity with their whole heart and soul. When I was a young man studying the blessed art of healing, this fact was indisputably borne in upon me by the loving care with which young physicians yet-to-be handled the dead bodies of their beloved kind in dissection rooms, that you, dear people, might have the benefit of their tremendous knowledge of all the strange and incoherent rivulets of life that a body contains."

His words came faster.

"In the divine process of nature there is no need of death. It only comes through defiance of nature's laws. Ignorant people often ask why the Great Ruler takes away the lives of little children, and so forth and so on. The answer is so simple as not to need an answer. It was the elders who in their crass ignorance neglected these children and failed to obtain for them the medicines which they so much needed."

He paused.

"But I wish to assure you, lad-ees and gentlemen, mine is not precisely a cure-all. You have many highly competent and courageous doctors in your most glorious city. Consult them by all means, and never lose sight of the God-given fact that the physician is your best friend. You must fain remember that our Blessed Saviour honored physicians by choosing one of them as a disciple—the learned Saint Luke of healing memory. I see you laughing over there, Brother. That is a fact. It is quite possible that others among the disciples were also physicians—for did not Christ say, 'Physician, heal thyself?' That has often been misconstrued in these later times. What the Saviour meant was that physicians one and all should heal themselves of little vanities and jealousies and work together for the good of mankind."

No rustic head turned. No movement was made. The tall man moved slowly up and down the platform, his hands behind his back, his head bowed. It had the effect of an old lion walking slowly and majestically before an audience.

The long arms went violently upward. He turned swiftly and faced the enraptured gathering of health seekers.

"I come before you as a friend, lad-ees and gentlemen, as one who bears the balm of Gilead out of Judea—the healer of hurt hearts and souls, of cold people huddling from the awful blasts of life and ever and anon shivering with the fare-thee-wells. I am the bearer of phosphorescent and beautifully burning coals of life—the healer who goes to out-of-the-way places and takes up the blistered and fevered agonies of men and gives them surcease. As I walked down the streets of your magnificent and beauty-laden city this evening little children followed me. It gave me meditation. A divine glow came to me. Inasmuch as you do it unto one of these so do you also do it unto me . . . My medicine encircles the world, I may say, to use a strange simile—children cry for it in many and diverse languages."

Heavily laden with bottles, Brother Jonathon's assistants moved to the rear of the audience. Seemingly unaware of their movements, his arms moving frantically, his eyes burning with hysteria he talked on.

"The friend of the family—the friend of the family! What blessed words! All our manifold blessings of civilization are built upon—the friend of the family. Unobtrusive, it is placed in an out-of-the-way part of the house. There, by the single movement of a little cork, the friend is ready to do your bidding —unobtrusive, demanding no attention but a small shelf upon which to await the summons when you are ready. As I say, by a simple movement of a little cork the gates of health and joy and peace and hope and dreams and the pursuit of happiness is yours, is yours. Yes, yes, by the simple movement of a little cork— not even a big cork—not one that sticks even, but scientifically arranged so as to fit the bottle and keep the precious liquid from the disintegrating rays of air and wind and sun.

"As Lonesome Ed Farley would say, the real pal is Giver of Life. All others may desert, but by the simple movement of a little cork you may open the heart of a friend. The heart of a friend—lad-ees and gentlemen, the heart of a friend—priced at two

dollars the wide world over—the heart of a friend
—now but *one* silver dollar, lad-ees and gentlemen,
but *one* silver dollar—a beggar's fee, lad-ees and
gentlemen, a beggar's fee!"

His hands flew upward again, his dynamic personality surging, his voice soothing.

"Now all together, lad-ees and gentlemen, let not
your right hand know what your left hand is doing—a
treat for the children, for the aged, and infirm—the
Giver of Life to them each and all! It takes the ache
from the tired mother's heart and back, it makes the
worn father a buoyant and cheerful provider of good
things for the entire family, it makes him sing at
his work and come home in the evening to his meal
like the boy you ladies loved ever and ever so long
ago when the sun was young and all nature was but
a benediction."

His rich voice crooned deep.

"Blessed are the meek, and the poor, and the
heavy laden, for from them shall the burden of the
world be lifted by the Giver of Life! For is it not
better to heal a soul that ails than to capture a city?"

Brother Jonathon extended his hands, palms downward, as though pronouncing a blessing. The audience sat silent.

His great voice was wrapt in velvet. The words
came in rolling fervor:

"I am the Great Healer,
I am the Great Healer,
I am—the—Great—Heal-er,
To heal you of your fears.

"How can you deny me,
How can you deny me,
How can—you—de-ny—me,
Who comes to you in tears.

"Mine is but the giving,
Mine is but the giving,
Mine is—but—the—giv-ing,
Of joy through all the years."

Calm thought was banished from the audience. Brother Jonathon stood still, his hands folded.

Voices were suddenly heard in all parts of the tent. Men bearing bottles were everywhere.

"Here it is—ladies and gentlemen—here it is! The Giver of Life! A small silver dollar! A small silver dollar! Doctor Maloney's great Life Giver!"

Money came from pockets. Never did prelate look more benign than Brother Jonathon.

Well he knew that it was hard to count money correctly in a whirl of many voices.

"Here it is! Here it is! A half-dozen bottles is not too many! It will be the last chance, lad-ies and gentle-men—the last chance!"

Clapping his hands, stamping his feet, shouting directions here and there, he allowed no time for the audience to "get set."

The bottle vendors also threw volleys of words.

He had often said to his helpers by way of instructions, "Nothing confuses people so much as counting money in public while others talk."

Seldom did Brother Jonathon fail in selling his medicine to the entire audience. They would walk out of the tent carrying bottles in hands and pockets. For the next hour Brother Jonathon would be busy settling accounts with his vendors.

Long after all had gone, he would remain alone. Stooped over an improvised desk, his eyes would peer closely at a cheap unlined paper tablet. A lead pencil would move feverishly in his talonlike hand.

Satisfied with the result, Brother Jonathon would place his hat carefully on his dismal yellowish-gray curls, adjust the lapels of his coat, and then his spats.

Pondering for a moment he would feel the small blue revolver which he always carried. His long fingers would wander to the wallet in his pocket and linger there.

He would then glance at the scene of his conquest and pick up his gold-headed cane and walk into the night—alone.

CHAPTER VIII
WAITING TO BE HUNG

The steady routine of the jail became very oppressive at times to the most dull inmate.

A loud whistle at an iron foundry would sound three times each day.

Through iron bars we would watch the army of laborers file wearily to and from their work. "They're all in jail like us," said Nitro Dugan.

"Only difference is they don't know it," called the pyromaniac.

"That's all the difference there is in the world— not to know things—it's knowledge that drives men mad—brick walls for brains to splatter against. It's all a mess, gentlemen, all a mess." Brother Jonathon watched the straggling workers with scorn.

"Maybe those birds made the bars that hold us here," suggested Dugan.

"Maybe they did." Brother Jonathon frowned.

"It was probably their uncles who made the spikes
that held the hands of Christ so lovingly to the cross."
His expression became more stern.

The whistle blew again calling men to labor.

The factory was so close to the jail that steam
could be seen rushing from the long-drawn blast.

At night when the whistle blew a chorus of voices
went up. "Another day gone."

They would count the times each would hear it
before they, too, were gone.

Joe Elvin awaited a new trial for murder. His features were effeminate, his hair deep yellow and curly.

He had escaped hanging twice. A new trial had
been granted him when he was being made ready to
march to the gallows. He had donned the clothes
without pockets and the worn carpet slippers in
which he was to die.

The guards had said to him, "All right, Joe. The
last day . . . write your letters an' say your prayers." The youth of twenty-three laughed in their
faces.

Each time the whistle blew Elvin would shout,
"Thank God, there'll be no whistles where I'm goin'.

"When I stick my head through the loop I want
a cheerful guard to go along with me. I'll never
forget how Wooden Leg Bill willed the warden the
shoe from his peg leg.

"The guard got excited when he was takin' him

up the steps of the gallows, an' Bill says: 'Don't get excited, Mister. There ain't no hurry. We gotta lot o' time.'

"Old Bill woke up the mornin' he was to be hung an' says to me: 'I won't wake up this time to-morrow. I'll be like the rich an' sleep late.' He's still sleepin'."

And Joe Elvin would laugh at the memory of Wooden Leg Bill.

The youth was petulant and full of snarls. Most of the jailbirds commiserated with him. He took the kindness of the worst human jackal with no more consideration than a spoiled child. Either having grown accustomed to thoughts of the dangling rope, or else death was to him of no concern, he generally dramatized it whenever possible.

Three of his early comrades had been hung. They all "died game."

"They'd kick me outta hell if I went there yellow," was his comment to Blink.

Elvin had one white mark on his black slate.

Before traveling the trail of murder he had held a rendezvous with a married lady at a cheap hotel. Five days later, he was arrested for a crime. He might have gained his freedom through an alibi. But that would have involved the woman's sorry little home.

He was given a ten-year sentence.

The woman went her way as before.

In the penitentiary Elvin told the tale to a convict

he had known on the outside. He was taking his punishment nonchalantly when the fellow convict wrote to the woman's husband.

That gentleman obtained freedom for Elvin—and for himself.

Elvin's mind always dwelt on the gallows.

The shadow of the noose was ever between his eyes. His thought turned suddenly and without warning to anecdotes connected with the instrument of legal murder.

"The warden came down Condemned Row before I left and I yelled at him: 'Say, warden, that was a dirty trick you played on us guys who're soon goin' to die. You let all the convicts see the free show the Salvation Army give except us—but you let everybody in to see our show . . .' An' he hung his head and beat it without sayin' a word."

Such tales generally created a lull in the jail conversation.

After this remark Gyp the Red asked: "Did you ever hear what the Reverend Simpson says to the lady reporter when he was about to be burned in the electric chair? Well, he says to her, he says, 'Madam, would you like to have my seat?'

"An' she says, 'No, thank you. I get off at the next stop.'"

"That's purty good! That's purty good!" exclaimed Elvin. Then his face went stern.

"That Simpson was the guy who bumped off the girl in the family way in Boston. Well, he deserved to croak, that guy did. Killin' a woman that way— anybody'll kill a woman, I say, bump him off. They don't deserve no mercy. I wouldn't pour water down a guy's throat like that if his soul was afire."

The factory whistle blew while Elvin listened.

Only by one story was Elvin ever visibly disturbed.

The tale was delivered by Brother Jonathon, as solemn as a funeral oration. All the cell doors were open.

There was a quality in the old man, blended of hauteur and effrontery, that brought him respect. Even Joe Elvin was less petulant with him.

Brother Jonathon was the first, and only great, Rotarian. In one way was he superior. The epitome of quackery in every form, he could laugh inwardly. He would express faith in all beliefs one day; deny them all the next. A chameleon of vagabond destiny, he was only sincere in his insincerity.

"You should prepare to meet your God, Joe, my boy," he said to the young murderer. "All men can't die like Bralen did, Joe—the phonograph record playing in his cell as he left it forever and a day:

" *'Come all you rounders if you want to hear,
The story about a brave engineer.'*

"Bralen didn't need to lean on God, Joe—but you *do*. Some men need God, and you are one of them. Bralen was the kind of a fellow who would have bawled God out for not letting it snow on Christmas. And maybe in the end, God got even. Now you don't want to take that chance, Joe. Put a bet on every horse that runs—then if there is a God up there, He'll reward you for being smart. A man never loses who hedges his bets enough, Joe."

Elvin looked at the old faker with pathetic reverence.

Brother Jonathon placed a hand on the murderer's shoulder. "Men die according to moods, my boy. Some strangle like gentlemen; others die like lawyers."

He looked into Elvin's troubled eyes.

"It was a very vast number of years ago that an Irishman and a Spaniard were sentenced to die together.

"The Spaniard had some strychnine in the cuff of his shirt. 'Here,' he said to the Irishman, 'I'll give you half—you can put it on the end of your tongue, and it'll save you dying like a dog in the rain.'

"The Irishman gave the alarm, but the Spaniard put the stuff on the end of his tongue and died in convulsions, like Cromwell on the road to glory.

"Both of them had killed an old woman for what they thought was a bag of gold. When the poor old crone was in heaven they found the bag was full of peanuts, and they, therefore, were full of chagrin.

"The Irishman went to the gallows quickly. He had confessed his sins to the priest, and he was in a hurry to die, so he couldn't commit another sin and have to go to confession all over again.

"It was a beautiful public hanging. It rained and thundered and the lightning flashed in mighty rivulets of gorgeous splendor. Hundreds of people stood in the rain to watch a beloved member of their blessed human race die.

"The trap fell, and the Irishman with it. The rope had slipped from around his neck. Both his legs were broken and he couldn't stand up, naturally enough, for how can a man stand with his legs broken?

"Hanging days were jubilee days in New Orleans then. The streets were crowded with people who ought to be hung. It took a hundred police to keep the mob quiet while they carried the man up to the scaffold and fixed the rope more firmly and securely around his neck. He whimpered like a baby who had not had a proper dose of Giver of Life. But this time it worked —and everybody shouted."

The old man had barely finished when Denver Shorty said, "Oh well—it was another stool pigeon less."

A weak smile died on Elvin's face.

The old man saw the pain.

"Death is nothing," he confided more cheerfully. "It's like going to sleep when you're tired."

Elvin's expression lifted. The old man continued.

"In England years ago they hung men in public for picking pockets. A crowd always turned out, and the pickpockets who were lucky enough not to be hung made more money that day than any other time. Many a purse was lost when the trap sprung.

"One time, the hangman strung up seven pickpockets. He got thirty-five dollars for the job—a guinea for each broken-necked thief.

"Well, he got all his money and left them hanging and hurried through the crowd. A pickpocket bumped into him and blew a breath full of garlic in his face.

"When the hangman came to he'd lost his thirty-five dollars and ten more besides. He never did regain his self-respect—a sad thing for a hangman."

Everybody laughed. Elvin remarked faintly, "Gee, that was funny." His mind was still on a gallows.

"Did you ever sell real estate, Joe?" Brother Jonathon asked.

"No," replied the youth.

"Well, I did. I went before the dumbest man in the world as a result.

"A lawyer of course is dumb, Joe, but a judge is a lawyer who failed. One cannot make a judge understand. For the minute a man understands he no longer judges.

"I happened in other days to sell some real estate for a living in California.

"An honest man, I was improperly brought before a tribunal for selling land which the buyer just as improperly thought was worthless.

"The man had the audacity to sue me for doing him the favor of allowing him to buy the land.

"He yelled loudly in open court, 'Your Honor, he told me I could grow nuts on that land.'

"The judge turned to me. 'Did you tell him that?' he asked.

" 'No, sir, Your Great Honor, I did not.'

" 'Then what did you tell him?' the judge asked sternly.

" 'I told him, Your Great Honor, that he could go nuts on that land.'

"The judge, like all lawyers, was envious of a man who had money which he had not stolen himself. I was forced, however illegally, to refund the man his money."

Elvin laughed more heartily.

A harmless old imbecile forever walked about the jail soft footed, like a man in a trance. Whenever he was within hearing of Elvin, he would exclaim, "That's right, Joe, that's right."

Elvin would smile and say, "You see, that old boy knows what's what."

No one seemed to know the nature of the old man's

crime. Skeletonlike, his eyes bulged so large in his bony face they seemed ready to drop from his head. He was precise and effeminate in manner. As a result, he was called "the old fairy."

He had a habit of gazing at a newspaper and pretending to read aloud. Distorted fancies crowded into his head. He enunciated slowly as the inmates pretended to listen.

To Elvin he always read tales of men who were hung.

They were generally more highly flavored tales which Elvin had first told him.

One had been the story of a beautiful young woman in England who had killed her fatherless baby.

As the hangman took her to the gallows he said softly: "Ah, dear, ah, dear! I'd rather kiss ye than hang ye!"

At different intervals the old imbecile walked about the jail, shaking his head and repeating the hangman's words: "Ah, dear! Ah, dear! I'd rather kiss ye than hang ye."

CHAPTER IX

A SAILOR LEAVES PORT

gallows himself. That may have softened his heart toward Elvin. For he was kind to him whenever possible.

The sailor was about forty-five years old. There was in his speech the twang of Vermont. He was reticent, solemn.

He had a frayed and filthy deck of cards with which he played solitaire by the hour. His eyes never left them. So concentrated was he that he had to be pushed off the bench by other prisoners when meals were announced.

He had been in all corners of the world. Once, when the bars of his reserve were let down, he talked with me one Monday afternoon. Brother Jonathon, Joe

Elvin, Blink, Denver Shorty, and Nitro Dugan soon joined us.

The bars and the sun that glinted through them were forgotten. He talked in jerks, with eyes half closed, in the manner of one who recalled memories but seldom.

Serving time for assault and battery, he had knocked three other sailors unconscious in a water-front dive. One man was expected to die. For weeks Burren faced the penitentiary. At last the man was declared out of danger.

Burren's face was as hard as a Vermont rock when he heard the news that freed him from a charge of manslaughter—and the Big House.

"He's a man, that fellow," declared Brother Jonathon, "he has the sea and the wind in his hair. This jail cannot affect him. Indeed it cannot, for 'Stone walls do not a prison make, nor iron bars a cage.' "

Nitro Dugan laughed sardonically.

"The hell they don't! What do you think keeps us in here—our shadows? Tell that to the guards—they're simple enough to believe it."

"But, Nitro—you must not take poetry so seriously."

"Well, maybe not," returned Nitro. "Get the Sailor to tell you the one on his dad—that's better."

We looked at the angular sailor.

Burren hated no man but his father. His teeth clenched at the memory of him.

"I'll never forget him, damn his soul! His mouth was like a trap you ketch rabbits in. His head was like an ostrich egg. He even tried to fool my mother when she was dyin'.

"I floated back home from Buenos Aires one time. We were all in a shack on the water front when in he comes. I had my back so's he couldn't see me— but I seen him in the glass.

"He says, 'Would any o' you men like to make five dollars?'

"I jumps up with a beard on me longer'n a Jew fiddler's hair. I'd been on a ship for months, an' the hair covered everything but my eyes. He didn't know me from Adam, for he ain't seen me in twenty-one years, and I says: 'Yes, mister, *I* would. What'll I have to do?' And he says: 'Nothin' much. You just make a dyin' woman happy—she's been a-callin' for her son till I got tired of it. She's near dead—so any woman's son'll do. You just walk in the room, and when she calls out "My Son!" you go up to the bed and say "Mother." '

" 'All right,' I says. So together we walked through the drizzlin' snow. I never says a word to the old geezer all the way to the house. I'd wanted to see my mother, but I'd wanted to wait till I got a ton o' whiskers off—but when I saw the old devil I jumped up anyhow.

"Well we got to the house an' I stood in the door and the old guy said, 'Mother, I brought your boy.' She reached out her hands and half moaned: 'My boy, my boy! I knew you'd come. Let's see the birthmark, son, let's feel the birthmark.' And I pulled open my shirt and let her feel a big welt on my breast that usta worry her. She closed her eyes and kissed me. It made me feel like a dog. But I says soothin' like, 'Lie still, Mumsy, lie still. I won't leave you.' An' she fell back on the pillow.

"I pushed her eyes down and turned to the old man and says, slappin' my breast, 'You see, I'm him . . . gimme the five.' He starts to hold back.

" 'Come on,' I says, and I twisted his arm around and took his whole leather wallet.

" 'Now, you old miser, you always would skin a gnat for its hide. This is *my money*—her share that you took. I won't even count it. I'll dress up to-morrow —an' you kin tell all the folks how I come home from a long cruise—an' that I'm a captain. An' when mother's buried I'll skin out agin—leavin' you to rub your mean old hands together forever . . .'

"Well, Ma was buried. The funeral was longer'n a whore's dream.

"I beat it in three days . . . and the old man and me never spoke all the time, damn his old soul!

"There was four hundred dollars in the wallet. I stayed drunk for a month."

Sailor Burren soon left the prison. He bade good-bye sharply. His lips were tight together as the jail door opened. Deep grooves were at the corners of his mouth.

After he had gone a silence of several moments hung over the jail.

CHAPTER X

AN OLD MAN IN MONTANA

Brother Jonathon commented.

"My own father was such a man that if a rabbit ran across his grave he would steal its tail. We had little in common.

"But he was a wily and witty man. He once made his brag that the earth was not large enough to hold Squire Devan and himself. The Squire was a dead shot —and penniless.

"He heard of my father's statement and sent word to him that he waited outside. 'Come out and get in the smoke,' he said.

"My father read the message and frowned. Then he said: 'I'm worth two hundred thousand dollars and the Squire isn't worth a cent. It would not be a good gamble.' "

The gathering of jailbirds laughed.

"At another time my father loaned a man fifty dollars. The man offered him security. My father refused. The man thanked him for his generosity. 'It's all right,' said Father, 'I don't want any security. If you don't pay me I'll kill you.' "

"I don't think the Sailor likes his dad," laughed Nitro Dugan. "He's just a little cuckoo, I suppose. It comes from bein' without women too long."

He looked at Brother Jonathon.

"Now, my dad was a different guy altogether. He was a chemist, and he had a system to keep kids from bein' born."

Dugan winked at Blink and watched the effect of the tale on Brother Jonathon.

The old man bowed his head.

"A filthy mind, Nitro, a filthy mind, you have."

"Well all I know is what Mother told me," said Nitro, winking at Blink.

"How could your mother discuss such a subject with you?" the old faker asked.

"Well, she probably didn't like to talk about such things with my two sisters."

The old man walked away, shaking his head. Laughter followed him.

"I know a yarn that beats the Sailor's." Denver Shorty's words followed the mirth.

Not over five feet, Denver Shorty had a broad face and broad shoulders. He had a pug nose, crooked eyes, and a limp in his left leg. His right hand twitched constantly, as though he were pulling the trigger of a revolver.

"I'll never forget one time when I was beatin' it through Montana," he began. "I was in a division point near Butte, and it was snowin' flakes bigger'n ostrich feathers. I went to catch a mail train on the Chicago and Milwaukee when a brakie throws a lump of coal on my head, an' when I come to the train was gone an' I was in a tool shed along the track with a guy over six feet tall an' older'n God.

"He was cleanin' monkey wrenches when I sat up, and he says, 'Lie still, young feller, the railroad dick'll be off duty in a little while now, then I'll take you home and you kin have breakfast at my house. My old lady said she'd have pancakes and molasses this mornin', and she can't be beat.'

"I wondered at first if he'd turn me over to the law, an' then I figgered I'd have to trust somebody, so's I said to myself I'll take a chance, 'cause it didn't make much difference whether I was in jail or on the freeze in the snow.

"I'd always been afraid of the town. She sure was hostile in the old days when Cherokee Sam was the railroad dick there. But they'd killed him one night and threw him under a freight . . . anyhow that's where they found him—on the track all cut up like cheap meat. There was a hole in his head a train didn't make.

"A buddy o' mine over in Great Falls told me that the new dick was just as bad as Cherokee Sam ever was—that he'd shoot a fly off an engine afore he'd let it ride without a ticket.

"The old man was a good geezer. He'd drug me into the shed outta the snow. He'd even put a blanket over me. When he got ready to go he says, 'Come on, kid,' an' I tagged along with him.

"The snow was fallin' so's you could hardly see it was mornin' an' we must 'a' walked along the track a half a mile before we turned in at a little house frontin' the railroad.

"The tiredest lookin' old woman you ever saw in your life met us. She had a red shawl around her, and a corncob pipe in her left mitt. It wasn't any bigger'n a crow's claw.

"The old man he says: 'Hello, Mumsy, brought a hungry kid home with me. Throw them pancakes on the fire.'

"Well, sir, the old lady starts to cookin' ham, an' you guys know how good it smells any old time— much less when you're cold and hain't eat in two days an' your ribs think they're jist a fence holdin' your guts in. The old boy fixes me up a place to wash, an' I left a ton o' dirt in the basin. A cinder'n my eye'd bothered me for a week, an' he took it out by wrappin' the corner of a handkerchief around a match.

"Then we sits down to scoff, and I never eats so much in my life.

"I says to him, 'Mister, you been here a long time, I'll bet.' An' he says: 'Yeap, son, nigh on to fifty years. I met my old lady when I first come here. She was workin' in a railroad boardin' house. She was purty in them days, weren't you, Ma?' 'Go on,' says the old lady, 'don't you josh the cook.' But she laughed tickled-like jist the same. Then the old man he laughs too, an' he says, 'An' she could cook even in them days like she kin now.'

" 'Gee,' I says after breakfast to them, 'I neved thought anybody'd be so kind to me in this town. I come through here one time three years ago, an' Cherokee Sam threw bullets all around me. I sure laughed when I heard they bumped him off, for he was a mean guy, wasn't he?'

"Jist then a freight made a lotta noise goin' by an' the old man didn't answer me.

"I knew the old boy'd have to sleep after workin' all night, so I thanked them an' beat it quick as I could after that. The old feller give me twenty cents.

" 'It'll git you somethin' warm a little later,' he says, 'you'll need it.'

"I hung around for a freight so long I near froze, so I beat it in the depot to thaw out an' I saw another tramp there.

"We got to talkin' like 'boes will, an' I tol' him of the good luck I had gittin' the ham an' cakes.

"He says: 'Oh, yeah—that old guy. A lotta the tramps are next to him. Him an' his old lady're peaches. Give you their shirts. They never turn nobody away.' The 'bo scraped a chunk o' mud an' snow off his shoe an' says: 'It's a funny thing, too—you can't beat it—the old man's part Indian they say. You know, their son was Cherokee Sam, the big dick the 'boes killed here. But they never let on.'

"I looked at the 'bo like I thought he was crazy.

" 'Do you think I'm kiddin' you?' he says.

"An' I says, 'No, but I'm damned if I'd ever feed a 'bo if one o' them had bumped my kid off.'

" 'No,' says the tramp, 'I don't think I would either—but I don't guess he figgers that way. They hain't no fool like an old fool.'

" 'I guess you're right,' I says.

"Then a freight train come, an' I left the other tramp sittin' there by the warm."

Denver Shorty twitched his right hand.
Nitro Dugan stood with mouth puckered in the

manner of a schoolboy trying to solve a problem in arithmetic.

At last he said, "*I knew* Cherokee Sam. He got what he God damned well deserved."

CHAPTER XI

BULL HORRORS

A HALF-DOZEN DOPE FIENDS MOVED FURTIVELY ABOUT
the jail. Their minds were in another world than the
one of steel which surrounded them.

They were known as "users."

Hypo Sleigh was the most picturesque of these.
He had been a heroin addict in earlier days. While
under the influence of this drug he became a burglar
and was sentenced to the penitentiary for some years
as a result. Due to that experience, he would not
now use heroin. Like all seasoned dope fiends, neither
would he use cocaine unless forced to do so by circumstances. He knew that an addict "loaded on C"
was subject to wild and painful imaginings.

His attitude recalled a murderer I had met on a
railroad in Texas.

The freight train jerked and rattled through the turbulent moon-drenched night. The wind sent the heavy smoke upward from the engine in magnificent white and black revolutions. Bright stars peeked through the whirling air chasms of smoke.

He had crawled into the box car at the last junction point. It was nearly dark at the time. Having beaten my way on the same train for over two hundred miles, I was tired and hungry and in no mood to talk.

Darkness crawled around us. It was soon banished by the moon. We said no word to each other for some miles.

The newly arrived hobo smoked one cigarette after another. He rolled them deftly with thumb and forefinger. He lit them with ease by scratching the match head with his finger nail.

I watched his face each time the flame touched the cigarette. It was like a rubber balloon that had wrinkled. It seemed to be always in hesitation between a snarl and a sardonic smile. His jaw was short and square. There was a deep scar across his chin. His eyes were somber and stared straight ahead. He had the oblivious manner of a person alone on earth. He must have been fifty years old.

His hands were powerful, overdeveloped. An upper tooth was missing. He held his cigarette in the vacant place. Each time he finished a cigarette he blew a ring of smoke and watched it circle to the roof of the car. He then stared straight ahead again.

We stopped at a siding to allow a faster train to crash by on its way to New Orleans.

We could feel the strong vibration of the ground as the train came mightily toward and beyond us. The lights from its coaches flickered quickly and disappeared from our open box-car door like lanterns carried by ghosts.

The noise of the rushing train became dimmer and dimmer. It at last died away and all became as silent as the falling petal of a rose. Then across the moonlit miles we heard the haunting music of its engine whistle. More mournful than the wailing of a lonely panther, it touched my youthful vagabond heart with sadness. I longed for the joys I had read of in books —but had never known.

The wailing music must have touched my fellow rover. He said, with a touch of despair in his voice, "That old rambler'll be in New Orleans in the mornin'." Then with a deep sigh, "I wish I was on her front blind."

"Not me," I replied moodily, "I nearly starved the last time I was there."

"Well, you'd starve in a bakery, then, kid," he said testily as he rolled another cigarette.

"Maybe so—but I washed dishes three nights in the Little Royal Restaurant to keep from it."

A light came into the man's balloonlike face.

"The Little Royal Restaurant, huh? Right around the corner from the St. Charles Hotel?"

"That's the one."

"I know where it is—I used to have a suite of rooms at the St. Charles in the old days—they were bigger'n a mint."

The memory seemed to please him. He whistled, his tongue against the roof of his mouth:

"Good-bye, farewell to Omaha, K.C., and Denver, too,
I got my foot on a flyin' freight, an' I'm goin' to ride her through.
Farewell to the boys in Illinois, and the girls on the Barbary Coast,
I'm back again with the hobo boys, an' the life I like the most.

"So long to the girl in Baltimore,
Don't ask me how I feel,
I got one foot on the heavenly shore,
And the other's on a banana peel."

The wind roared louder. Clouds of white and black smoke scurried through the open door of the car.

Silence followed the wind. Footsteps could be heard on the graveled roadbed.

A voice asked, "Which way, 'boes?"

My comrade half mumbled, looking straight ahead, "Down through Texas."

The man swung into the car.

"Don't you know you can't ride this road without money?" he jerked at us.

He wore a corduroy suit. His cap, of the same material, had a heavy piece of aluminum across the back. He carried a railroad lantern.

My comrade sat, hunched up, his forearms across his knees, his back against the side of the car.

"I suppose so," he replied.

"Well, you supposed right," shot back the man. "I'm runnin' this train, and your tickets are punched at this station." He waved his lantern toward the door. "Pile off!" he yelled.

I rose to my feet with tired unconcern. My companion did likewise. The man glared at us.

"Where are we?" I asked.

"None of your business—who cares where two tramps are?" snapped the conductor as I walked wearily toward the door.

"Well, I care where *one* tramp is," snarled my comrade.

I turned quickly.

The vagrant stood within two feet of the conductor, who held his lantern half poised, a look of horror on his face. A blunt revolver was leveled at his heart.

"Now where are we?" commanded the hobo.

The conductor explained in shaking detail, "You're on the Houston and Texas Central Railroad, Mister —a-headin' into Fort Worth."

"Have we got a clear track?"

"Yes, sir," replied the conductor.

Then quickly—"Here, kid, I'll take his watch an' coin, an' you take the con's lantern and wave a high ball from the door—do you know how?"

I answered in the affirmative and waved the signal for the train to move. It was soon on its way.

My companion then snarled to the conductor, "Come on—git off!"

He then whistled with soft menace:

"Jay Gould said before he died,
He was goin' to build a road the bums couldn't ride,
And if they rode they'd ride the rods,
And place their lives in the hands of the gods."

He stopped whistling suddenly and yelled, "Jump off!"

The conductor hesitated.

"Come on, come on!" urged the man with the revolver. "Suppose this gun goes off before you jump?"

He flourished the weapon. The conductor jumped.

We watched him sprawl and rise as the caboose passed him.

Turning to me—"Lord, what a strain that was! But I'll not walk for any man." He shrugged his shoulders. "I've taken orders enough in my day."

I looked out of the car. The smoke came thinner and whiter from the engine. The moon shone brighter. We lapsed into an intense silence. Again the vagrant smoked cigarettes swiftly, then spasmodically, then not at all. He began to fidget and removed his coat. He then sat still for a minute and rubbed his bare, needle-scarred arms. Little blue marks were all over them. His shoulders moved nervously. Then he sighed deeply between gusts of rising wind.

He bent double before me. His face took on the painful expression of a badly punished pugilist awaiting the gong. Though still a boy, I knew what his agony meant.

"Did you ever take a shot, kid?" he asked.

"Nope, I never have, but I'll help you if you want me to."

He ignored my offer, but his face became kinder.

"Well, don't you ever take one then, kid, because if you never start you'll never have to stop." He rubbed his eyes. "There ain't no stoppin' . . . not if you bite your fingers off—and your heart aches till it stops." His voice reached a high note and subsided softly. "I know—good God—I've tried!"

His hand trembled, and his entire body shook.

The wind died away.

Then as if defending himself—"You know, kid, I had a shot before I got on this train—that shows what nerve kin do. I'd kick the moon outta the sky, boy, when I'm loaded. That's the kind of a fellow I am."

He fumbled in his coat pocket and took from it the small tin lid of a typewriter ribbon box. He filled it with a powder which looked yellow in the moonlight.

His hand shook so violently he could hardly hold the lid.

"Let me hold it for you," I volunteered.

He handed the lid to me without a word. His mind seemed far away. He fumbled in the coat pocket again and brought forth a small bottle of water.

"Gotta always watch out—didn't have this water I'd have to use my own spit," he said half to himself as he poured the water over the powder and stirred it with the end of a match before lighting it.

The blaze flickered under the small lid and heated its contents of dreams.

After it became warm he sucked it into a small glass dropper and threw the lid down carelessly. He then pulled a piece of quarter-inch rope from his hip pocket.

"Hold it around my arm, won't you, kid, so's the pain won't shoot up?"

He handed me the rope. I wrapped it once around

his arm below the elbow and held with all my strength.

He felt the flat part of his wrist above the palm of his hand.

"I ain't hardly got any more veins to shoot in," he said dolefully. Then, locating a spot, he made a quick incision with the end of a large brass safety pin.

He shot the dreams into his arm, and I released the rope.

"Ah . . . ah!" He breathed deeply.

His pain-shriven face became radiant.

It is impossible to mistake the effects of cocaine for those of any other narcotic. Many of the older addicts feel that shooting it in the body gives better results than sniffing it. The effects do not wear off so soon when it is shot into the body. A sniff will last about fifteen minutes; a shot will last a half hour and often longer.

Cocaine produces a feeling of unlimited self-confidence and tremendous bravery. It sharpens the faculties to an oftentimes indescribable alertness. It has been known to give inarticulate men conceptions of grandeur worthy of a Milton—for half an hour. They then subside—the cracked shells of eggs from which eagle dreams have flown.

My comrade's body stiffened. It was as if a fierce electric current had been sent through it. He sat erect.

"You know, kid, when I was ridin'—before the big trouble come—I wouldn't look at a plug that couldn't do two hundred miles a minute—why, Lester and Johnny Reiff and Tod Sloan used to be my stable boys in them days! I was a rider, I was . . ."

He hit his chest.

"I could ride 'em bareback—any old way. I just left a circus in San Antone two weeks ago." He threw his head back, his eyes dilated.

"The circus boss got tough at me, and I says to him: 'You ain't got nothin' on me, you crummy old circus stiff! I tramped in every state in this country before I turned jockey and the big trouble come— why, I know more about horses than Brigadier Young knew about women!' Then he called me a little drink o' bad water and I did get sore, and I says to him: 'I'll turn your fat old elephants into snakes and I'll make 'em pull your circus away. An' I'll turn your lions into rabbits.' He got fresh some more and I did what I said; and, sure enough, you should of seen them elephants crawl away with that circus! They were bigger'n whales crawlin' . . . and the little lions were all rabbits squealin' like sucklin' pigs. I kicked the whey outta them. An' all the time the big elephants crawled away wit' the circus . . . like big, long snakes, only they had elephants' heads . . . and when they'd hiss they'd blow the ground away for a hundred feet under them. Then the silly fools'd have to crawl through the holes they'd made and drag the circus after them. We sure had a devil of a time.

"I shipped the elephants to New York an' sold 'em to Barnum for eighty million. The boss runs up to me like a little boy an' he says, 'You won't take my pets, will you?' And I says, 'Gwan away, or I'll brain you.' He bellers, 'You wouldn't hit an old man like me, would you?' 'Yes, you're cockeyed right, I would,' I says. 'I'd hit Tom Thumb wit' a broad ax.' He didn't bother me no more, and I hain't seen him since."

He rubbed his eyes.

"I jist got outta Shreveport three months ago. I done twenty years straight. It sure was a tough break. An' kid, the night o' the big trouble you should 'a' seen me. I plugged her perty, I did. I says, 'Listen, little girl, I'm goin' to let your soul out,' an' I spit the bullets through her double-crossin' heart, an' she tumbled like a paper sack wit' the wind gone out of it. She'd took me over the hurdle for all my dough. I went on the hop for her. Then, when I couldn't ride no more, she wants to give me the high sign an' run away wit' a travelin' salesman. Then I loads up on heroin—and when she sees me comin' wit' her hearse in my eyes, an' the horses trottin' fast to her graveyard, she screamed an' I says to her: 'Say your prayers, little girl. You're agoin' home to die no more.' "

The vagrant broke into a loud chant:

"To die no more, to die no more,
  You're goin' home—to die no more,
  To die no more, to die no more,
  A little blonde angel forevermore."

He rose, raised his arms high, staggered once, then seated himself hastily.

"That's what they git for foolin' wit' me!" His voice sank to a dismal guttural.

"And when she lay there all dead—a splotch of blood on her white waist—I fell down over her an' moaned: 'Oh, kid, oh, kid, for God's sake! I didn't mean to do it. Come on back. We'll git outta here an' beat it to New Orleans . . . this town never was no good . . . ' I rubbed her cheeks, I pried open her eyes. Then my lights went out, an' I musta slep' wit' my hand on her heart—for it was all bloody. When I got away, for over a week I loaded up all the time on morph' an' coke—a-sniffin' it till it'd go clear down to my belly an' roll my brain over.

"I went to a flop at a little hotel, and outta my window was a pulley where they used to lift trunks up in the old days. There was an old rope still hangin' on it. I locked myself in an' loaded up some more— an' all the time I was afraid of the cops.

"I'll never forgit the dreams I had in that room. I took six or seven bangs of coke an' floated away to Chicago, China, an' the North Pole. Then I beat it out of there an' down the street, an' I saw a tent in a window an' I stood there catchin' fish bigger'n whales, wit' two tails an' four heads. Every time I'd pull one outta the water I'd knock a buildin' down. When I got tired fishin' I sat on a box three feet high in front of the store, an' I looked up at a tall buildin' across the street. I counted all the stories to the very top—forty-eight o' them—an' out of every window a blonde girl fell with blood all over her heart. I tried to light a faggot—then I watched the match burn up—then I saw it fall forty-eight stories an' start a tiny blaze around every blonde girl's heart —an' all the girls looked alike, jist like my little blonde girl . . . an', God, she was a peach . . . body like white velvet! Then I lit all the matches in the box an' watched 'em float down—one by one like a lotta stars—all of 'em my little blonde sweetheart wit' blood splotched on her breast. . . ."

The train rattled on. The lights of Fort Worth were more clearly reflected against the sky. He talked on.

"Then I looked up an' saw two cops watchin' me . . . an' it was jist my luck that I had to pass through them to git away. Then a hundred more joined 'em an' they all wore masks an' they all had red spots where their hearts were an' I could hear 'em beat out loud. They made such a noise they near drove me crazy. If you ever hear a million cops' hearts beat like hammers you'll know what I mean.

"Finally a fellow comes into the room an' says, 'The bulls are after you, pal, so jist lay quiet . . . there's only a million of 'em, an' the chief's along.' His eyes was red as ripe tomatoes with little green holes in the center. He turned the key soft, an', Lord, how I screamed! The guy was a liar . . . there was two million eighty-eight hundred cops. I counted 'em as they stood in the door!

"They lined up two hundred thousand a piece, like the spokes of a wheel, an' the big chief stood in the center like a hub . . . an' they begins to circle around an' around . . . so fast they was nothin' but blurs like an electric fan . . . an' I runs to the chief an' blew my breath an' he fell down dead. Then I shot twelve times . . . right straight down the line each time . . . I'm a fiend for shootin' through people's hearts . . . an' I plugged the whole line. The bullets zipped right through all their hearts, even their coats turned into red an' blue an' green blood . . . an' it stuck 'em all together like big, bloated, blue sardines standin' up straight. The whole wheel stopped dead still. They held their clubs up in the air like little tin soldiers.

"Then I got up on the bed an' gives 'em a talk.

'Listen, you big blue whales,' I says. 'If you'd 'a' gone to work like honest men you wouldn't be dead now. You thought you was goin' to hang me, did you? Well, the rope ain't been made that'll string me up, an' the man ain't made that's big enough to spring the trap after the rope's been made.'

"Them two million cops began to grin like a lotta pawnbrokers in heaven. But the eighty-eight hundred don't grin—they just put their fingers to their noses. I didn't mind that, but I sure knocked them two million loafers under the law, down flat. That scared the dickens outta them for a minute—me, a jockey, knockin' two million of 'em down! You know, they're all yellow anyhow . . ."

The engine whistle shrieked for a crossing. The train slowed suddenly as if about to enter a railroad yard. It soon gained momentum.

The vagrant's hand shook. He stared madly. He laughed shrilly.

"Then all them two million cops began to laugh agin, an' they all got up an' marched laughin' out loud in twos and twos in an' outta the window, walkin' on the air, an' singin': 'You thought we was dead, did you, buddy? Ho, ho, ho! Ho, ho, ho!' An' the bed shook from under me where I sat. They formed in line agin like a wheel . . . an' I blazed twenty-four bullets down the lines o' their hearts. The blood spurted all over the room, an' they laughed still louder.

"'I'll fix you, you blue bloodhounds!' I says. 'I'll shoot you through your heads.' An' first I shot their hats off—an' they all took the beaks an' wings o' buzzards an' flew purty as death aroun' the room. I looked up an' saw them flyin' way up near the stars right close to the ceilin'. Then I pulls the trigger twelve times through all the spokes o' their skulls . . . an' they kep' on laughin' an' their brains seeped out like long white ropes an' circled aroun' their necks, an' they all looked like a lotta big blue fish in a net all tangled up. 'Ho, ho, ho!' they laughs. 'You thought you'd shoot our brains out when we ain't got any! If we had brains we wouldn't be cops!' An' they laughed like a lotta ravens an' in a minute they all fell down dead . . . an' the buzzards lit on 'em. Then I got scared an' begun to run an' got tripped up in their ropy brains that was all over the place. An' I fell down an' a buzzard pecked me in the back o' the head an' says, 'Come on—get outta here—you ain't dead yet . . .' Then those dead cops begin to laugh an' all say at once: 'Why, ain't he dead? He's jist carryin' hisself aroun' till we git the scaffold up.' They scrambles up on their feet an' kicks the buzzards away, an' begins shakin' their heads. An' their brains begin to roll back in their heads like thread on an empty spool.

"Then the guy comes agin an' put his cap over the doorknob so's no one could see through the keyhole. Then he whispers low like:

" 'They're after me too, kid—'cause I murdered two million o' them. But they won't git us. We'll float outta here to-night an' be in Paris in the mornin'.'

"My pal's nose was long an' crooked an' he only had three teeth in front of his mouth—an' it was bigger'n Roosevelt's. Then he sits down on the edge of my bed an' brings out a small brown can from his shirt and yells louder'n thunder at me, 'Get the scoop!' Then he took a large nail file from the end of his belt that didn't have no buckle. Then he lifts the lid from the brown can an' brought out a lot o' silver sparklin' cocaine on the end o' the file. He holds his hand under the file so's not to lose the least bit. I heard him snort like a lion—then he gives me a sniff.

"Then we heard men walkin' in the hallway an' saw someone stickin' somethin' through the keyhole to knock my pal's hat off the knob. Then some cops looked through the transom. Then somebody crashed the window open. We both ran to it an' looked down. I'll bet you there was ten million more cops climbin' up that rope an' jumpin' into my room. No lyin'! I tried to push 'em away . . . an' they broke the door down, an' I'll bet twenty million more comes in that way an' they all kep' yellin', 'We want you, buddy! The jig's all up—the rope's all ready—got it greased nice an' slick so's it won't burn your neck. We gotta boy here who'll tie it right back o' your left ear so's it'll jerk your head purty an' you won't never know you're dead.'

"I yelled out loud, 'Git outta here . . . an' lemme alone!' An' they all laughed till the bed fell down again. I looked around for my pal an' he was gone. The cops kep' on laughin' an' the walls caved in.

" 'Now,' I says, 'look what you went an' done. I don't own this shack.'

" 'No, but you might as well,' they says. 'It's jist a boardin' house fer crooks.' 'I ain't a crook,' I says, 'I'm the best jockey that ever lived.' Then they all laughs some more.

" 'Come on here, buddy! We don't want you for bein' a good jockey. The little girl had as much right to live as you. You wasn't her judge an' you had no right to kill her. Come on, buddy, it won't take long. The rope's waitin'. We'll have the chief say mass over you, and you know when you make your confession you go to heaven anyhow. All you gotta do is bump somebody off an' tell the priest an' you go right to heaven.'

"Then they all laughed out loud agin an' I yells, 'Git outta here!' An' I started shootin'. Then somethin' fell on my dome, an' my lights went out agin, an' I woke up in jail."

He turned suddenly pensive and stared into space again.

"An' the funny part of it is . . . I don't know yet what it was all about. I learned later that there wasn't a bull in the room. An' if I'd laid off the heroin I might 'a' got away. But I did twenty years."

He tried to roll a cigarette and failed. He threw paper and tobacco on the floor and said, "Anyhow, the little blonde double-crosser's doin' from now on . . ."

The force of the man's tale made him crumple for a moment. Remembered pain stared from his eyes.

The wheels rattled over the intersecting rails. I looked out of the car and saw many tracks; they glistened under the lights of swiftly moving engines.

"Let's beat it from the train," I said. "You've got the con's money and watch, you know."

The vagrant turned suddenly toward me. "Beat it if you wanta!" he shouted. "But I'm goin' to run this train to the moon. I gotta railroad watch an' everything!"

The train's speed rapidly diminished. I swung low, jumped to the ground, then hid behind a box car until the caboose passed.

The rear brakeman signaled to the engineer. Knowing that the conductor would soon be missed, I hurried across the tracks toward Fort Worth.

I had no qualms. The law of the road was the law of life—to save one's self.

The conductor would find his way home, I mused. He would get another watch and have another pay day—maybe.

CHAPTER XII
THE GRAVEYARD THAT MOVEL

Sleeping or waking, hypo sleigh was seldom still for a moment. Well known in the underworld, he was in jail for selling drugs to other addicts.

His name was derived from the fact that when under the influence of a "whizbang," cocaine and morphine mixed together, he would ride millions of miles over endless valleys of snow in a sleigh drawn by camels hundreds of feet high. They traveled faster than bullets when first leaving the gun.

Often, in the midst of a tale of men moving snow with shovels larger than Chicago, he would show his jagged teeth in a smile and tiptoe to the door and listen intently for the police.

"They're all outside in the hall, but they can't get in. Can't you hear them marching and laughing?

They're hanging the chief—thirty thousand cops right outside." Then he would resume his tale.

He claimed to be the son of a Winnipeg doctor. As a youth he had accompanied his father often in a sleigh to see patients. These incidents may have been frozen in his mind.

Why he was not confined in an asylum is one of the mysteries of government.

His mind was fantastic, his mouth crooked, his teeth yellow, sparse, and snagged. The top of his head was completely bald. In nervous moments he would rub it with a handkerchief until it shone like a mirror. Then he would rise and sing:

> *"I got a great big automobile—*
> *With diamond headlights and a golden wheel—*
> *I ride to heaven and there I pray—*
> *And then I jump in my silver sleigh—"*

He would patter his long feet on the floor in tune with the words.

Hypo Sleigh was an object of pity to all in jail. Like most pity, it was wasted.

For he could play poker with the King of Siam and win a million dollars with the first card that came to his hand. He could make the King pay it in nickels and dimes, and then he could spend an hour counting it ten thousand times.

He could twitch the King's nose and exclaim, "Listen, King—when I lose—I pay everything . . . you are a nickel and a dime short—pay it or I'll kill every Irish nigger in your kingdom." The King, in tears, would send to a golden and diamond studded vault for the fifteen cents. Hypo Sleigh would give it to the poor.

When too destitute to "make a buy" or when "stood on the corner," the dope peddler not making an appearance, Hypo Sleigh was a man of such imagination that he would seek other addicts and tell them marvelous tales until they would give him a "jolt."

Hypo was always a talker and a man of action. He robbed banks with Jesse James. That handsome ruffian did Sleigh's bidding for thirty-eight years. Hypo had put a bullet in his heart. "Every time he threatened to leave me, I'd tell him I'd pull the bullet outta his heart and he'd die."

Hypo Sleigh once, with the help of Jesse James, robbed the Bank of England. They had the money taken to their rooms in eighty patrol wagons. Policemen were made to guard the wagons. They robbed the robbers.

Jesse James cried over this misfortune until Hypo threatened to remove the bullet from his heart.

He once made arrangements to go to China. By such a journey he felt he could eliminate the middleman's profit in opium.

While under the influence of a drug he was re-buffed by a flunky in uniform at the door of an exclusive hotel.

He struck a dignified attitude and exclaimed, "Sir —I've been adjudged insane by many competent authorities, and if I should have the good fortune to kill you this moment I would be allowed to go free."

The flunky apologized profusely.

Hypo Sleigh entered the hotel.

He once sold all the sheep in Golden Gate Park to a visiting rustic from Iowa. Hypo Sleigh gave him a receipt for his money. It was signed Jonathon Swift Armour.

If dope could not be obtained in the jail Hypo Sleigh would smoke marihuana. Webster calls it "a narcotic plant reputed to cause insanity in persons drinking an infusion of its leaves or smoking them."

The Mexican convicts called it "Greefo." Hypo called it "muggles."

It is a loco weed which grows in the Southwest. When eaten by cattle it causes them to become temporarily insane.

Hypo's muggle cigarettes were cured in alcohol and dipped in perfume.

One cigarette affected his brain for as long as six hours.

It distorted his vision and gave objects a far-off appearance.

It caused mirages of beauty and terror to dance before his eyes.

It would produce senseless laughter at the most unexpected moment.

It caused Hypo to imagine that he was dead. He would caress a fellow jailbird in the belief that he was a woman who would not be able to see a dead man.

After a long smoke Hypo would imagine he was dying and at the same time walking up a steep hill.

He would lift his feet constantly as if stepping over large rocks.

At other times Hypo Sleigh would assume postures of great dignity and loudly exclaim: "Unhand me, officer. Do not touch the President without his request." He would brush his sleeve with meticulous care.

He walked up and down the iron enclosure of the jail, muttering and gesticulating. Suddenly he stood still and looked at the barred window high above his head. No ray of sun came through.

He twitched his long fingers. Then he rasped so that all could hear:

"It ain't no use to grumble and complain,
It's just as cheap and easy to rejoice . . .
When God sorts out the weather and sends rain . . .
Why rain's my choice."

By some unknown source he was well supplied with his favorite drug.

He rubbed his head feverishly. He then laid the handkerchief carefully on the floor and talked to the ceiling.

Jailbirds, anxious for diversion, gathered about him. He waved his hands . . .

"Gather around me jailbirds while ye may . . .
Your time is still a-flying. . . .
And he that is in jail to-day . . .
To-morrow will be dying."

Dippy the pyromaniac stepped close to him. He watched him with curious eyes.

Hypo assumed a dramatic pose.

"For he was my enemy, men. He jerked the rope as I stood on the gallows. But it was not around my neck. It was around his own. His sister died for love of me, and the judge accused him of killing her. And when he died the warden said he was glad to tell me that he was dead. I told him I was sorry. But I went to the morgue and claimed the body. That is my own father, I told the bookkeeper of the dead. He was a scientist. He died to test a rope.

"So I took his body away with me to a medical college.

"Young doctors with smiling faces and long carving knives gathered around me with blood in their eyes.

" 'Another man has died for humanity,' they said. Feeling happy at the thought of selling the body of my enemy for money and science, I laid it carefully before them.

"They looked at it as longingly as a damsel looks at the fool she loves. Their fingers itched on their knives. Finally the eldest of them yelled in a horrified manner: 'We cannot use this body. It would mar our abstract tendency at the circumlocution of the heterogeneous matter in the bicepereous end of the nose. For you see, fellow members, it has a long wart.'

"Now here was I with the body of my enemy, trudging down the street sadder than any man. His ears stuck out of my pocket, and I couldn't put them back.

"A policeman started to chase me yelling louder than Grover Cleveland, 'Hurry citizens . . . the man is stealing a mule.' I ran as never mortal man ran before. Suddenly there was a fearful noise as of thunder. A million mules brayed in a meadow. The noise roared out of my pocket and broke my eardrums. They fell in pieces on the ground. I only eluded my pursuers with the help of night that wrapped its black mantle in undulating folds about me.

"Staggering and tired, with the ears of mules wriggling out of all my pockets, I sat down to rest.

"A man bigger than a tree and glowing like a lightning bug tapped me on the shoulder.

" 'You must bury that body,' he roared.

"A streak of lightning followed his words.

" 'But the body does not belong to me,' I screamed. 'It is my enemy and therefore a jackass and not my father as I claimed.' The body glowed till it hurt my eyes. Then its mouth opened like a cave. He blew wind and laughter. A flame flew from under its tongue.

" 'That does not matter—let the dead past bury its dead,' he said. 'I make you the keeper of the long silence; the guardian of meadows eternal where jackasses wallow in grass of illusion until they become angels. Hurry with the body to the nearest graveyard—for much will happen this night that has never happened before.' I started away—'And hold . . .' He held up a finger bigger than a log. 'Dig deep the grave—fifty-eight feet and two inches—place it directly beneath the largest tree in the cemetery . . . and if roots get in your way you must bite them in twain with your teeth—for I'm getting God damned tired of the lies of men in the world who steal bodies and souls.' The death sweat was on me, I was so scared.

"I hurried away with my ear flapping burden and reached the graveyard. I could hear people talking under the ground.

"I dug four days and four nights and ate away the

roots of the tree and placed the body of my enemy in the hard ground. It was midnight and I was tired.

"Then the fool's ears grew longer, and I had to dig six feet deeper. They kept growing and growing till my spade wore out.

"I went mad and cut the ears off. It showed my ignorance of biology. But how was I to know that if you cut off a mule's ears in a graveyard that it will rouse the dead? I happened to remember that my father, who was a doctor, never cut off a man's ears in his life. But it was too late then."

Hypo Sleigh pondered, his forehead wrinkled, his eyes closed. He resumed quickly and dramatically. His eyes were now as startled as if he really stared at ghosts.

"Before I could think, the dead were all around me. They walked like skeletons and yet they had flesh on them. Their bodies glistened, and their bones were as shiny as dice in a nigger's hand. One skeleton was a young woman, not over twenty-four. She was dark as a Russian princess and her hair was gold. Her eyes were big and brown. She looked like a lady who had just died. 'So you cut off a dead man's ears,' she whispered. '*You poor man.*' She shuddered. 'The one sin in all the world you should not have committed.' She sighed very deeply.

"I tried to run. Not a hand touched me. I could not move. Something cold as worms crawled up my legs. I heard a horrid braying. The ground trembled. Mules ran through the air. Their ears swished back and forth.

"My enemy galloped out of the grave and across the headstones. His dripping ears covered the ground with blood. He ran braying across the river. His hoofs splashed the water over the graves that lined the shore.

"A lot of other people jumped out of their graves and yelled after him: 'Hey—what the hell do you think this is—wetting our graves in the middle of the night.'

"The girl with the gold hair said very softly to me, '*Too bad!*' She trembled all over. 'Like people on earth, I worry over the sins of others and forget my own. What a crime you've committed. You brought the man to life eternal by cutting his ears off. You are a *murderer!*'

"I fell on my knees. 'Most beautiful of women . . . he was my enemy.'

" 'There is no such thing,' she said. 'Enemies are merely people who do not understand.'

"She frowned prettily. 'Why did you not refrain from cutting off his ears? Why did you not leave him to rest? He was securely dead and away from the ills of earth.'

"Other ghosts gathered around me. They rubbed

their left and right forefingers as little children do when they shame each other. I became enraged and struck at them. My hands went through them. Their bony hands slapped me, knocked me down.

"Then another fearful braying was heard. My enemy dashed back across the river and came snorting toward me. The girl with the hair of gold looked at him.

" 'Be gone among your kind,' she commanded. Away he sailed across the river again. The ghosts at the edge of the water threw stones at him. One hit him on the tail. I laughed out loud. A ghost knocked me down again. I rose unconscious.

"An old ghost came up to where we stood. He had been out of the world a long time. He was dressed as a soldier who had fought in the Revolution. He had a yellow sash and a dead rose on his chest. He looked like the pictures of Andrew Jackson after he'd had trouble with women.

"He blew a little horn. Ghosts came running from all directions. They stood in a big group in front of him. One ghost pulled a worm from another's ears. They all chortled.

" 'Fellow citizens of the Long and Blessed Silence,' the old ghost yelled, 'we have been here, some of us, nigh on to three hundred years. We have seen America grow into a most amazing country, the greatest in the world.' The audience applauded. 'No longer does the Indian maiden linger on our graves, nor the Indian lover say the world-old nothings under the moon.

" 'In the old days our graves were sacred. Then, youthful skeletons-yet-to-be had the woods and the meadows in which to beget future skeletons of gratified desire. Crowded out of those places now, they come and make immoral our beds. They rob us of the rest which we have so richly earned. For were we not once youthful skeletons-yet-to-be like themselves?

" 'Death, as we have learned, is the peaceful, the sweet, the hopeful, the everlasting. Citizens of another world, strangled men, shot men, women dead with unborn babies, no mockery of religion and no religion here, no wild passions that tear the heart to shreds, no unfulfilled desires, no women crying in the night, no chatter of heaven, no fear of hell, no warbling of fanatics, no fools, no definitions of things that can never be known—nothing but peace, with the gentle worms and the roots of sunflowers in our ears.

" 'We ask no boon from the turbulent people who put us here. For we are the living and they are the dead. They talk of beauty and eat dead hogs for breakfast, while we feel the throbbings of worlds in the crumbs of dirt about us.

" 'We can hear the strongest oak coffin crumble with the noise of an earthquake. We can lie in our beds and hear the moans of dying snobs who are soon to find equality for once in their lives. We can see brains that have swayed worlds shrivel like the guts of dead cats. And it is just as well. For one makes the strings of violins, and the other sadness upon earth. And, in the end, even we cannot tell them apart.

" 'At first when we arrive here, we are worldly. In a hundred years, or such a matter, our dust becomes more refined. You who are but recently dead should fain remember my words. But as we go on in death our ears become more sensitive. Often we listen to the music of silver bells a thousand miles away. We can hear death touching a girl upon the shoulder a year before she is aware of it. We can hear the nails going into coffins before the trees which make them are cut down. We can hear undertakers charging five hundred dollars for a thirty-dollar pine box with cheap pale blue plush around it.

" 'We can hear them say to the half-starved widow, "Yes, madam—we must respect our dead." And we laugh—knowing that the dead cannot respect them.

" 'We can turn on our sides and see the armies of millions marching and marching forever. They blaze past the sun, their skeletons shining like the faces of maidens in love. They carry the instruments by which they died—bayonets, bullets, daggers, poison, love, hope, fear, and platitudes.

" 'They carry more—starvation in their bellies and ignorance in their heads. They carry guns that belch at other men, and purses stolen from others. They gyrate around the moon, they copulate with other maggots and beget other maggots that die in time and become skeletons that march in front of the blazing sun. And what for—gentlemen and lady ghosts—that yokels might procreate other yokels on our graves and theirs while they march in front of the sun and die in the rear of the moon.'

"Suddenly the old ghost's speech was interrupted. A hearse came out of a flame with the body of a judge inside. It rumbled loudly and stopped in the midst of the assemblage.

"The judge got out of his coffin and addressed the speaker with deference. A ghost with a broken neck and a red mark in the back of his left ear saw the dead judge. He placed his long fingers carefully on the neck of the dark girl with the hair of gold.

" 'Make him take your hands off your neck, dear girl,' the ghost with the red mark behind his ear exclaimed. 'For he sent me here before I was ready to come. The hangman he had me say, "Our Father who art in heaven . . ." and before I could finish the sentence he sent me to the Man I thought I was praying to.' The ghost felt the red scar on his neck and ran with menace toward the dead judge. Before anyone could stop him he pulled a sharp knife from a hidden pocket in a bone and cut the judge's ears off. The judge turned into a jackass at once. He began to bray. 'Live forever,' screamed the ghost who'd been hung, 'forever and forever. Keep flying and running.

" 'Your soul is too black to lie under a white tombstone.'

"The blood dripped in rivers while the jackass that was the judge brayed. Suddenly he ran, a mass of red, and splashed into the river.

" 'Run your damn' fool head off. You'll never be able to stop. I cut off your ears close so you'll run forever. Run around the world from now on and jump over every gallows you see. You can't eat hay and you can't eat corn—and all you can do is suck wind forever.'

"A torrent of blood fell over us. The jackass ran like the lightning and brayed like the thunder. His braying shook a rib from the side of an old ghost leaning on a marble slab."

Hypo Sleigh held his arm circled and poised for a moment, as if it were about a person to whom he talked.

"So you lost a rib, did you?" he laughed. "Well— so did Adam."

He dropped his arm.

"Now run along—I'm talking."

Hypo looked upward.

"The man who'd been hung threw a rope and caught the jackass around the head. He held onto the rope and jerked himself on the back of the mule. It snorted, reared on its hind legs, plunged through the air, and rolled over on the graves. Still the ghost of the man who'd been hung stayed on his back. He beat the mule over its stubs of sore ears with the end of a club. The blood spurted more and more.

" 'What a hell of a life you're goin' to live forever, judge,' the man who'd been hung shouted. 'I'm goin' to ride you an' ride you forever, and I'll beat your sore ears till the blood turns to chunks of liver in your head. And even then you won't be able to die. And when I get tired I'll let all the other men who've been hung ride you two at a time.'

"The jackass brayed as if its heart would break. The rider on its back yelled as they circled around us, 'They who condemn men to die by the rope shall never have the solace of death by the rope—no one but ghosts can see them . . . but all the men who've ever hung men are circling through the skies forever— jackasses with their ears cut off——'

"The mule dashed into a white cloud and turned it bloody red. The old ghost started to talk again.

" 'It is time we moved from here, fellow gentlemen and ladies. Our graves have been too long molested by youth planting human seed upon them.' He waved his bony arms. 'Let us cross over the river and found a great new city.'

"An army of ghosts formed millions of miles long.

"I did not see an ugly woman ghost among them. Death seems to turn women beautiful. They danced past me as graceful as maidens strewing flowers under an April moon. They seemed rested. For no woman among them was in the family way.

"They crossed on a barge that crossed the river.

"Not even after a great battle was there ever such a gathering of ghosts.

"They gathered on the barge by millions. The air swarmed with them. Their transparent bodies shone as if phosphorescent. Even the red and white corpuscles in their blood could be differentiated. Only, their blood did not flow. Their hearts were still.

"A large ghost with a lantern jaw and a vicious expression fell heavily on the barge.

"A sound, as of falling débris, followed him.

"A group of ghosts ran toward him. 'Are you hurt?' they asked.

" 'No, thank God, I'm dead,' he answered, rubbing his right hip. 'However, I did make an awful mistake.' There was silence on the barge.

"Above was a droning sound as of millions of bumble bees.

" 'What was your business in the nether world?' a young lady ghost asked.

" 'It was not a business, lady; in the classification of my occupation I would prefer to differ with you.'

" 'Ah . . .' her face became demure.

" 'Mine was a profession, lady. I was a bank robber.' The bones of his chest rattled as he patted it.

" 'How fearfully dramatic,' the young lady ghost exclaimed.

" 'It was indeed—a fearful profession. I'm afraid I left my comrades in the lurch.' A sad expression crept into the bank robber's eyes.

" 'I had it all arranged with the sheriff and the chief of police. They were to be playing poker with Reverend Sanctus, the leading reform minister, and Mr. Grubbins, Superintendent of the Y.M.C.A.

" 'These gentlemen, being engaged in an innocent pastime, would thus leave the bank unprotected.

" 'I was to rob it at midnight and divide the spoils with these gentlemen.

" 'Everything went merry as an Irish funeral. My plans were perfect. I had a bottle of nitroglycerin carefully ensconced in my hip pocket. The money glittered in the safe before me as I began to crawl into the window.

" 'A feeling of piety came over me.

" 'I glowed to think of the great good that Reverend Sanctus and Mr. Grubbins could do with the money should I be weak enough to divide with them.

" 'Reverend Sanctus had told me that God was the only Man who could trace the sources of money—that robbing Peter tc pay Paul was really an apostolic maxim written in heaven by Judas Iscariot in a moment of inspiration.

" 'I was halfway through the window. It very inadvertently came down on my right hip pocket.

" 'This would have been merely a slight accident. But, alas—it contained the nitroglycerin.

"There was never such an explosion. It tore the wings from the angels in heaven. Blood from lovely shoulders dripped on the white locks of Moses who debated with Cesare Borgia and Joan of Arc on the origin of sin.

" 'The explosion destroyed the whole town. Being nearer to the scene of the accident, I naturally left first.'

"A group of rough appearing shades quarreled to the rear of the bank burglar.

" 'Aw, shut up,' one said, 'don't hand me that stuff —you'd bite a worm if it got too near.'

" 'The uncouth children of gratified desire,' murmured a bespectacled and shriveled shade with a book in his hand.

"He had no sooner spoken than a flying ghost knocked him sprawling. 'Another piece of whalebone that crumbled at last,' said the shriveled shade, gazing at the newly fallen ghost whose fingers twitched as the breath gathered in his throat.

"The bank burglar rubbed his right hip.

" 'Why, hello, sheriff,' he exclaimed to the new arrival.

" 'Don't talk to me, you blundering fool,' returned the sheriff. 'The next time I want a bank robbed I'll have Reverend Sanctus do it.'

"Before the bank robber could reply another body crashed on the barge.

"A battered badge clattered on the floor.

"The bank burglar trembled as he recognized the chief of police.

"That infuriated gentleman picked up his badge and pinned it to his coat. He then pointed angrily at the burglar and yelled: 'Officers, do your duty. Arrest that man.'

"The barge rocked with laughter.

"The sheriff approached the chief. 'Don't you know where you are?' he asked.

" 'No,' replied the chief. 'Where the hell am I?'

"The sheriff mused for a moment and smiled.

" 'Well—you're dead—but you wouldn't know that. You've been a policeman too long.'

"The chief looked startled.

" 'My God—*dead*—what'll become of my poor wife?'

" 'Don't worry about her,' a ghost chuckled, 'she'll marry a desk sergeant within a year.'

" 'What became of Reverend Sanctus?' the sheriff asked.

" 'He was playing cards with Mr. Grubbins when I left,' replied the chief.

"The barge glided, silent as sunlight, over the silver river.

"Police chief, sheriff, and bank robber watched the distant shore.

"It had nearly faded from sight when a cry of consternation went up from thousands of ghosts.

"A beautiful sheep-eyed youth had fallen overboard.

"There followed wailing and weeping.

"Many screamed, 'Help—help—a man is drowning.'

"The old ghost leader peered into the water.

" 'It is no matter,' he said with light voice. 'Let him drown—it is only recently he died for love.'

"The barge soon reached the other shore.

"Large billboards faced the river. The words glared in electric lights.

This Is

VALHALLA

The California of the Dead
New Site for

THE CEMETERY BEAUTIFUL

Be Kind to Your Loved Ones
They Are Not Gone—but Absent.

"The old ghost read the words and exclaimed, 'Oh my God!' "

Hypo Sleigh stood as erect and still as stone. For an instant his eyes seemed petrified. They protruded, yellow and blood streaked.

Then over his body passed, like a shadow from the sun, a wave of softness. His eyes and posture became normal.

The door of the jail opened. A guard entered with another prisoner. Hypo Sleigh looked intently at them.

"Which is which?" he asked. "Which is which?"

The guard frowned. The inmates smiled.

No jailbird answered.

The incendiary chortled.

CHAPTER XIII

A LIGHTER OF FLAMES

Dippy had always been a pyromaniac.

At five years of age he was taken to a Fourth of July celebration at the county seat. The skyrockets blazing heavenward in many colors made him ill. He went into a spasm. His mother took him home.

His father owned a farm in an Eastern state. During summer nights the boy would stand as in a trance and watch the fireflies darting over the meadows and the hills.

At six he would steal matches from the kitchen and build small fires in the woods at the far edge of his father's farm.

His imagination early sensed the power of a match.

"It would get to be a blaze as big as the world right in my hand."

When a vivid calendar picture of a forest fire came to the home he begged for it with such energy that his mother gave it to him. It hung over his bed.

It made such an impression on his mind that he tried to burn a neighbor's woods on the day it arrived. The underbrush, being either too green or too wet, he was unable to duplicate the scene in the picture.

The delight of his childhood was to help his mother build fires in the kitchen stove.

It soon spread over the country neighborhood that the boy built all the fires in the house.

Neighbor women shook their heads over the folly of giving so young a boy so great a responsibility.

On winter evenings the future incendiary would watch the parlor stove burn dull red with heat. His mother would often notice his intense expression as he gazed at the stove.

"What are you thinking about, Son, are your lessons too hard?"

His eyes never leaving the stove, the boy would reply, "No, Mother."

When he was eleven years old his father put a wire fence completely about the farm. The rail fence, which had stood for years, had been torn down. Filled with dry rot, it was not fit for fuel.

The boy burned the rails in piles. So engrossed was

he in the labor that he would not hear the dinner bell at noon. The hired girl would go after him.

He asked his father's permission to be allowed to work late at night in burning the rails. When enveloped in darkness the flames had a greater fascination for him.

The mania increased when he reached the age of puberty. Early that year he burned the barns of two neighbors. In each instance he hurried to his home and remained there until the blaze lit up the countryside. Then, knowing that the fire would attract people for miles around, he returned to the scene.

Late that summer a tramp passed the boy's home. The father allowed him to sleep in the hay loft. With the memory of his neighbors' barns in mind the farmer searched the vagabond to make sure that he had no matches. Convinced that the derelict was harmless, the farmer sent his boy for a horse blanket and helped the vagrant into the loft.

The barn burned that night. The old tramp, horrified, ran down the road. He was captured by a neighbor and taken to the county jail, where he remained many months until mistaken rural justice was satisfied.

The youth watched the fire with avid pleasure.

The intensity of the mania left him for some years. But he dreamed of fires always.

Hell was to him a roaring mass of flames. Fire

wagons rumbled over the road past his home to the hell of his imagination many leagues beyond. Fireflies larger than owls flew over the immense blaze.

A burning moon, miles wide, hung in the sky. The youth heard burning trees crashing and falling out of the dead planet. The flaming orbit would swing across the heavens like the pendulum of the clock in his mother's kitchen.

Firemen resembling those he had seen in pictures would chop with blazing axes at burning trees in the moon. Sparks larger than the houses flew from their axes. The lights from the eyes of the immense fireflies would make the scene more vivid.

At nineteen he fell in love with a neighbor's daughter. His passion for the girl became as overwhelming as his desire to start fires.

The maiden was in love with another farmer. She did not respond to the young pyromaniac.

On the evening of the girl's wedding her father's house burned to the ground.

Rustic bride and groom and rustic guests and minister hurried outside. The rejected suitor and his parents were in the group.

The lighter of flames watched the bride with deep concern as the blaze illuminated her features.

"My father didn't talk all that night nor the next day, neither," said the pyromaniac. "He watched me at the fire, an' I knew he thought somethin' was wrong."

In a few days the father asked his son to accompany him to the county seat.

What the father thought will never be known. The richest farmer in the district, he may have worried about damages.

"You had better go out West in a few weeks," he said as they rode along. "Bid your mother good-bye quiet-like and say nothin' to nobody else. I'll give you a thousand dollars—but you mustn't come back."

The youth obeyed his father.

Over thirty years had passed. The pyromaniac did not know whether his parents were alive or dead. Neither did he ever say in which state he had lived.

Captured at twenty-four, he served five years for arson. The name he gave to the police was not that of his father.

Released from prison, he secured work as a railroad fireman. He followed this labor for three years. The hours were long, the work hard. He did not complain.

"I loved to see the coal burnin' in the box. I'd 'a' been there yet—but somethin' happened," he said ruefully.

He fell in love with a brakeman's wife. She repulsed him. Setting fire to her house, he leaned against a telephone pole and gazed as intently at the flames as he had at his mother's stove so many years before.

The expression on his face made it so obvious that he was the incendiary that even the police were not mistaken. He was easily captured. Proven guilty, he was given another term in a state prison.

Attracted by the pyromaniac's docile nature, the warden made him his special messenger and trusty within two years.

As illiterate.as a sea gull, the prison official believed that religion and repentance could turn even politicians and convicts into angels.

He turned the Salvation Army loose on the unprotected inmates. They held meetings at every opportunity.

The noise of the drum, the fife, and the clarinet made religion a necessity to the more sensitive inmates.

Ever the fool of fire and love, the poor pyromaniac became infatuated with the one female member under fifty of the soul-saving band.

All of Dippy's women were of fair proportions physically. The middle-aged lady who shook the tambourine was no exception.

Like jelly that never properly settled, her body quivered constantly. She waddled when she walked.

But her mind, if not firm, was pure. She tried to lead Dippy to the Golden Gate of God.

During the days of his conversion the woman of God often read the Bible to the lighter of flames.

He was enraptured each time the word fire was

mentioned in the ancient Book of fables. He leaned close as the woman read:

"And Abraham took the wood of the burnt offering, and laid it upon Isaac his son; and he took the fire in his hand, and a knife; and they went both of them together.

"And Isaac spake unto Abraham his father, and said, My father! And he said, Here am I, my son. And he said, Behold the fire and the wood; but where is the lamb for the burnt offering?"

It was not long until the demented jailbird found justification for his career in the words of the Holy Scripture.

Like most men of more gross affairs, the pyromaniac's mind was balanced between earth and heaven. Having been touched with the gift of fire by his Creator, he was naturally much interested in hell as pictured by the lady colonel of the Salvation Army.

Her moron mind drew pictures of that place worthy of the arch fanatics, Dante and Milton. The lighter of flames listened piously while imaginary conflagrations seared his brain.

Each night, before slumber came to the tormented man, he saw a lady waddling through fire with a tambourine. As usual, his passion for fire and female developed simultaneously. Hour after hour he suffered on his narrow iron cot.

He formed in line for breakfast each morning. No more bedraggled and forlorn individual ever groped through the chaotic illusion of existence.

The fat lady rattled her tambourine in a blaze at the edge of his tasteless oatmeal.

He visualized flames wiping the warden's antiquated residence away.

Love, however, frustrated his evil design.

The next Sunday morning in chapel he ran down the aisle and caressed his heavy inamorata.

Everyone in the church was astonished. The lady wept tears of joy.

The warden looked up from his meditations of piety and frowned.

The culprit was taken away. He spent the next twenty-four hours in solitary confinement.

He was given bread and water next morning and taken before the warden, who, still stunned by what he considered the prisoner's ingratitude, pronounced sentence.

An iron chain and ball was fastened to each of Dippy's ankles. He was placed in the center of the penitentiary yard with an iron wheelbarrow. The iron balls were placed in the wheelbarrow. They were still attached to the chains.

A guard sat on a chair. For eight hours each day

for two months Dippy wheeled the iron balls in the barrow around the guard. He carried them with him to his meals and to his cell at night. The riveted iron band infected his left ankle. It ate to the bone and shortened the leg.

Dippy was not without solace. The woman of God remained loyal to him.

She made rainbows of his chains. Sparks of fire flew from them as he thought of her.

She married Dippy upon his release.

Prison life had so undermined the pyromaniac by this time that he was unable to earn a living. His wife laid aside her tambourine and took in boarders.

Dippy's sad world opened to the lilting of larks. Altogether too happy for any man with a diseased brain, he built the fires each morning, ran errands, and waited on the table.

In five months he became jealous of another ex-convict whom his wife was shielding from sin.

He burned his own dwelling. His wife was caught in the flames and died before Dippy came to trial.

The news of her death distressed him deeply. He screamed during the night, until a trusty dashed water in his face. He dreaded water like a cat and suffered in silence thereafter.

During his sleepless nights he would often rise in the manner of one against whose will beat impulses he could not control.

Each drab morning found him nervous and hysterical. Later in the day he became more irritable, and then depressed to the verge of hypochondria. The jailbirds gave him more understanding than the prison officials. To relieve the boredom of the jail they talked to him constantly.

A prisoner said to him one afternoon, as the sun threw barred shadows across the floor, "Dippy, you'd be happy in hell."

The pyromaniac's face became clouded.

"No, no—I like blazes that don't burn people. I'm not God or the devil." He rubbed his hands nervously. "I only like to see horses burn in barns." Then ecstatically: "Did you ever see horses burn?"

He looked jubilant and answered his own question.

"I *did*. It was me that burned my father's barn . . . he musta knowed . . . he musta knowed." With braggadocio: "It was the biggest fire in the county. Horses never move from fire. It curls around them an' burns their tails an' manes . . . swift. I think it makes 'em cool.

"They put their heads on the mangers an' close their eyes. Then they lie on their sides an' the blazes run down their throats an' cooks their hearts. They squeal a little bit an' stretch out."

Then, twisting his gray hair: "Trees always grow better on horses' graves that have died in blazes."

His audience looked incredulous.

"That's a fact," emphasized Dippy. "I seen lilies grow on top o' the two trees my father planted on our horses that died . . . I remember.

"Now a mule," went on the pyromaniac, "they're different. You can't burn a mule. It'd tear down the China wall to git from a blaze."

Dippy heard a match strike and looked around.

"A lion's like a mule. It won't go near a fire. But *me*—I love 'em."

He returned from the courtroom with dazed eyes and blue lips that quivered.

We gathered around the pyromaniac to learn of his sentence. He was too befuddled to talk above a whisper.

"Did you git it all, Dippy?" asked an impatient jailbird.

"Jist as bad," he answered, "twenty years straight. The judge said he was sorry he couldn't hang me. He said I'd killed my wife an' I never did. He called me mean names." His voice became stronger, his body drooped more. "It'll be the end o' me—hard labor and slow death for twenty years. . . ."

"Maybe not, Dippy—maybe they'll let you burn the pen down," suggested Denver Shorty.

"That's right, Shorty, that's right," the Old Crow, the stool pigeon, snickered.

Stooped nearly double, with lecherous defeated eyes

and bloodless, nervous, and bony fingers, the Old Crow leered at the newly elected candidate for the Big House.

"Twenty years, hey Dippy—the warden'll git to go to your funeral. They'll stick you in a cheap pine coffin an' the bottom'll fall out afore you git to your grave."

He laughed at the pyromaniac.

"You'll be a hundred an' nine in twenty years. The captain o' the guard'll have to strike the matches for you. They're allus kind to a goofus when he gits old in the pen."

Nonplussed, Dippy looked at the Old Crow.

"If I thought you was kiddin' me I'd git mad." He said the words slowly.

The Old Crow leered with mock benevolence.

"Kiddin' you, Dippy—who could do that! An' they'll lose you, Dippy, on the way to the graveyard. The warden he'll say: 'Where the hell's that damn firebug—he'll be burnin' his own coffin if we don't git him buried soon. I saw him slip a match in his pocket afore he died.' "

"Well, I hain't an old woman, anyhow." Dippy's words were acrid.

"You hain't—hain't you? Well, I'll betcha when they git you up there they'll give you a skirt—*now you see*. You kin write a letter to my lawyer an' tell me if it ain't true. . . ."

"Don't let him tease you, Dippy," Texas Gyp said. "He's jist tryin' to git your nanny."

"He ain't a-gittin' my nanny, an' he ain't a-teasin' me. They can't no old woman bother me none—they gotta be younger."

"Well you would'n' bother the young ones none," the Old Crow retorted.

The lighter of flames turned his eyes away.

"Maybe so—but I've been—but it's no use. Why don't you go on about your knittin'? Ain't I got trouble enough facin' me without your lip? Suppose you was me, you wouldn't feel like braggin', would you? Spillin' all that truck about me burnin' my own coffin—you know the warden wouldn't say that. *After all*, how could I burn my own coffin? I ain't a witch. You're all the time sayin' things . . . a-shootin' off your bazoo like I was a murderer or somethin'. Seems to me the judge said enough to me for one day. You ain't him, an' you ain't God, neither. You ain't nothin' but jist an old thief an' stool pigeon with a lotta rusty screws loose in your head. You belong in a nut house, an' not here among civilized men."

Dippy looked scornfully at his antagonist.

"An' I ain't a stool pigeon, thank my blessed Saviour. I ain't never told on anyone in my life."

The Old Crow ignored the last words with, "Well I

ain't so nutty I'm bein' sent to the pen for twenty years for burnin' people's buildin's down."

Dippy's head went back with disdain.

"It takes brains to burn buildin's down. You'd git your own self caught afire if *you* tried it."

Jailbirds, highly pleased at the repartee, spurred the decrepit verbalists on.

"Don't let him kid you, Dippy, he's always lippin' in," Denver Shorty cajoled. "If he had half your guts they'd be sendin' him on a twenty-year stretch."

"You bet your life, Denver." The pyromaniac looked appealingly around. "He ain't got no right talkin' to me thataway. If I want any o' his lip I'll ask him. He ain't the judge—even if he is an old woman."

Brother Jonathon looked from one recalcitrant wastrel to the other. Then all three old men exchanged glances.

"Why can't you two men love each other . . . you'll soon be separated a long time," the aged peacemaker suggested, folding his hands.

"The longer the better," put in Dippy quickly. "He ain't got no right to pick no quarrel with me— he ain't never even gimme a match in his life."

"What's more—I hain't never goin' to, neither. You been given too many matches—that's the trouble with you." The Old Crow made a motion with his bloodless hands. "They should roll you down a

hill in a barrel o' water an' put the blazes out in you."
He stood erect as possible. "That's all that's wrong
with you. You got blazes where your brains oughta
be. Your mother musta been on fire the night you was
born."

The last sentence was the undoing of Dippy. He
trembled, as into his dazed eyes came the terror of
remembered love.

His tongue pushed his blue lips apart. It remained
between them for a moment, as though he were
mustering strength to pull it back.

"You should'n'a said that—you should'n'a said
that." His words were soft as falling snow.

"Said what?" snapped the Old Crow.

"Them last words." The pyromaniac touched his
blue lips again with his tongue. "You'll never have no
luck in the world so long's you talk that away to
people."

He looked kindly at the now viperish Old Crow.
"It ain't my mother's fault 'cause I was born. She
wanted a baby girl, anyhow. You should'n'a insult
men's mothers—they ain't to blame."

The life-whipped incendiary sobbed forlornly.

"You'll git your pay for this, Crow, you jist see
if you don't."

Old Crow started to talk.

Gimp the Red, always a sentimental desperado,
applied what is known as the "strong arm" to him.

His right arm locked the Old Crow's head in a vise from behind. Purple faced and strangling, he was dragged away and thrown in a heap on the filthy floor of the jail. Gimp brushed his arm and returned to the group which still stood about the sobbing pyromaniac.

"I guess that done him some good," the strong arm artist ejaculated, "when they git to talkin' about a guy's mother—that's out."

The lighter of flames, still weeping, thanked effusively the man who had taken his part.

"Don't thank me—thank my bringin' up, old boy. I guess they ain't none of us so low but what we got sisters an' mothers." A smug expression crawled over his hard face.

Nitro Dugan said nothing. He merely watched the proceedings with a smile of contempt.

The next batch of prisoners would leave for the penitentiary in twenty-four hours. The lighter of flames would be among them.

"I ain't used to it yet," he confided to Nitro.

"Well, you light the fires wrong, Dippy. You hold your mouth too straight when you strike the match. I've been watching you in here."

The derelict of blazes took the words seriously.

"Do you think that's so?" he asked.

"Sure it's so—you'll never git caught if you hold the match in water a minute before you strike it."

The pyromaniac listened intently.

Eddie Evans lit a cigarette. Handing the match to Dippy, he said, "Blow it out."

Instead the pyromaniac held the match as though it were a rare jewel. Forgetful of the next twenty years he watched it burn to nothing between his fingers.

The next day at dusk he left for the penitentiary. Handcuffed to another prisoner, he resembled a tatter-ed wraith into which life had been indifferently fused. He suffered with his mouth. It twisted in many shapes.

His one shoulder drooped even lower than usual. He held his head turtle fashion, to one side. He scraped his feet on the sheet-metal floor in the manner of a punch-drunk pugilist before the gong sounds. The gray hair no longer straggled. He had twisted it into ropes. They projected from his head. His eyes had no more expression than those of a student of divinity.

A few men were locked in their cells for infractions of rules. The rest of us wandered about the immense steel room.

Now all looked at the door out of which would soon go frayed miscreants of crime to the penitentiary.

Deep pity is not the chief virtue of mankind either in jail or out. With the exception of the Old Crow, the crudest among us pitied Dippy.

"He's nuttier'n a guard," was the common opinion.

Denver Shorty tried to hand him surreptitiously a small box of matches. The guard knocked it to the floor.

Dippy watched it fall with protruding eyes.

We looked kindly at the ghostly incendiary. For we who had no buildings to burn had found him only a source of amusement, and often of gentleness. He was greedy of nothing in the world but matches. Like most men with a fixed idea, he was loquacious. It was a virtue in jail. It served to lighten the tedium. For, whenever the hours brought misery and longing for freedom with them, we would talk to Dippy.

"Step lively, lift your feet!" the guard commanded.

The other prisoner jerked the handcuff which attached him to Dippy.

The lighter of flames took his empty and pitiful gaze from us to the heavy steel door. Bolts slid. It clanged open and shut.

Dippy was gone.

"The poor fool," Denver Shorty said.

"He ain't got brains enough to be a fool," returned another prisoner.

"Well, anyhow, it ain't safe to let guys like that

run loose," volunteered a burglar. "He's liable to burn your house down while you're sleepin'."

"You're sure's hell right," said the pickpocket. "Everybody's better off with him in jail."

The iron bell rang for the evening meal.

The insane traveler to the penitentiary was soon forgotten.

CHAPTER XIV
FAITHFUL UNTO THE END

EDDIE EVANS HAD DRIFTED EARLY TO THE CABBAGE Patch. He was one of those children thrown up on the great shore of life with a potentially sweet nature and an embittered heart. He hated judges and juries and all the blundering instruments of injustice.

Nothing good ever came out of Cabbage Patch. The young women turned into whores; the young men into pimps, procurers, bootleggers, poolroom vagrants, and thieves.

It stretched along the lake, with the railroad tracks between. The pine houses, eaten by smoke and whipped by wind, were the color of burned slate.

The Cabbage Patch stultified everything within its borders. Its citizens were degraded, snarling, vicious. So terrible was the weight of its atmosphere that its most beautiful women looked old and haggard at thirty. Their breasts went flat, their cheeks sunk in, their skins turned sickly yellow, their hair smoke be-grimed, their lips twisted with sneers.

They resembled prematurely old and once beautiful witches who had drunk too early and deep of the bitter water.

The lake was a revel of beauty under the moon and sun, and a whirling and seething panorama of drama in snowy and stormy weather. It was not for the dazed citizens of Cabbage Patch. The endless tossing of the edges of its great blanket of water against the shore was like a requiem for the blighted souls of its citizens who had died in embryo.

In summer weather the children played wearily on the streets beneath shadeless trees that had long since died. Their elders sat on the doorsteps—perspiring, dirty, vacuous, hopeless, and forlorn. Their children, fit answers to those who talk of heredity as a greater force than environment, were listless replicas of their life-beaten progenitors.

Eddie's father had been a blond of immense pro-portions. Many women loved him deeply, including his wife.

Untrained in biology, she had the usual notion that a lion of sex must conform to the rules of a kitten. For the welfare of society that was perhaps the right attitude. It worked havoc with the sire of Eddie Evans.

His wife shot him through the heart.

Eddie was seven when it happened. His chief comfort at the time was his mother's sister. His Aunt Alice was sixteen.

His mother took veronal immediately after the event. She lay unconscious many hours and then joined her blond husband.

They buried the father first.

Eddie crept into the room and pleaded, "Daddy, Daddy, you're just playin' sleepy—you're not dead—you'll come back to me." He put his little hands on the white dead face and touched the forever combed hair the color of his own.

Evans had been a well-liked man before the bullet came.

Hundreds of telegrams had arrived on his wedding day. They wished him joy and a long, happy married life.

He was on a far road as a salesman. His salary was twenty-five thousand dollars a year at thirty-eight. His line was—imported lingerie.

A man who more than paid his way, he was always in debt.

Alice put her arms about her nephew and led him from the coffin. She was more beautiful than her sister's child, and more delicate than a humming bird. Like vitriol in a rare Sèvres vase, there was hidden in her nature the seed of her ruin.

Episcopalian platitudes followed Evans to the grave.

There was also a large gathering of people. Like most men quickly forgotten, Evans was popular in his lifetime.

He had a habit of telling his intimate cronies the names of ladies with whom he had been intimate.

Seven of these women stood about the grave with their husbands. Their eyes were tear stained as he was lowered into the earth.

They were faithful unto the end.

CHAPTER XV

LOVE FINDS A WAY

Eddie was eighteen, with yellow hair and wondering hazel eyes. Too beautiful for a boy, his life in the prison was made a constant hardship by sex-starved men. They made efforts to caress and fondle him whenever possible.

Always they failed.

Eddie was not pure so far as sex morality was concerned. He did feel, however, that he was not common.

He was effeminate, coy—a girl in many respects. The emotion that ruined his mother was not lacking in himself. It was under a terrible control.

Like all effeminate youths, Eddie liked to be treated as a masculine equal.

How could he, with a banker for a willing lover, become intimate with men in jail?

The gentleman of finance had made violent love to the beautiful boy. He won Eddie's affections—with interest.

Eddie blackmailed him systematically for years.

I early learned of the banker's sad romance. He was an obese pillar of a rickety church. Nature, the greatest of ironical gamblers, is never without a Joker in the deck.

She gave the banker lynx cunning and a hyena smile in making interest accrue. She married him to a woman who believed the world was made in six days. That she could not even unravel the tangled tinsel cords in her husband's nature in that time did not concern her.

To give a religious banker such a devout wife and a love for boys might have been enough, even for nature.

But to throw a boy like Eddie Evans in his way . . . it was enough to make the gods roll over the clouds with laughter.

No lady was ever more merciless in a love affair than Eddie.

His lack of gratitude toward the banker was the

cause of his incarceration. He was booked on a simple vagrancy charge.

Had he been accused of blackmail, the banker would have been forced to suffer. The devious channels through which money flows in the nether world will not be traced for some years.

The gentleman of finance was negotiating with Eddie through a lawyer skilled in such transactions. Eddie was promised freedom, a large sum of money, and a one-way ticket to Australia.

Eddie took several days in which to make up his mind. He did not like to go so far away from his protector.

Another young boy had entered the jail. He became quite friendly with Eddie. He, too, was not normal sexually.

He was as normal as a woman, however, in the fact that he could not respond to every type of man.

He had forged a check for a small amount.

He had gone into a clothing store with the check. When he handed it in payment the cashier asked him to wait. An hour passed. Still the lad waited.

Feeling certain the check was being investigated, he lacked the courage to bolt out of the store.

"I couldn't move," he said, puzzled. "I'm a timid person."

"But you had the nerve to go that far," I said to him.

"It was all the nerve I had—I couldn't move." He made a pathetic gesture. "Finally the detectives came and got me." He looked at our steel surroundings. "The first night here I'd have killed myself if I could."

I understood. Then I said, by way of encouragement: "But things will be all right. The worst is over."

He looked dubiously at me.

He was volatile, yielding, and charming. Similar to Eddie Evans in many respects, Willie Richmon lacked the hardness that would make him survive.

Girl-like, he looked about the jail with wide, whipped eyes. The rugged masculinity of one inmate appealed to him. He became attached to Nitro Dugan. That brigand was in his own words "a woman hound." He had no prejudice against such boys. "I'm just not left-handed," he used to say.

Dugan was the only person in the jail who could touch the boy.

Brother Jonathon looked upon sexual aberrations with abhorrence. But he treated both Eddie Evans and Willie Richmon with all the kindness with which an old priest would two wayward girls. And like the priest, while he did not understand, he was compassionate enough to leave all such matters to God.

"He's a good old man," was Eddie's estimate of the old medicine faker.

Life was full of worries for Willie Richmon. His parents were deeply religious and poverty-stricken members of one of the oldest creeds. He did not like girls. To please his mother he accompanied one everywhere.

A gentleman high school principal, as queer as the boy, had fallen in love with Willie. The youth did not respond. The teacher persisted.

When the boy was arrested the teacher came to his rescue.

Men of the law felt that the boy's parents had not looked after him properly. He was given probation—under one condition. That he live with the teacher and remain under his moral guidance for two years.

"I hated to tell him that he was repellent to me— so I used to tell him that I respected him too much to let him touch me," Willie cried petulantly, and stamped his foot like a mad little girl.

Eddie Evans was hard.

"You can always run away and go to someone you like," he said to him.

So the youth finally decided that living under such conditions was better than going to the penitentiary.

The judge told him that he should feel thankful

to God for so loyal a friend as the teacher. Thus another strange union was made in the world.

It was considered a heroic action on the part of the teacher. Maiden ladies, advisers of the young in other departments of the school, gathered in the courtroom. The benignant principal posed for a photograph with the boy. He stood erect, shoulders thrown back, strong arm linked in the arm of his youthful charge. The young forger had a crestfallen expression, like that of a maiden whipped by circumstances into wedding a man she did not love.

Several cynical young jailbirds smiled at the picture next day. A picture of the boy's mother was in a small insert beneath that of the teacher. We looked solemnly at the woman's harrowed face and pondered.

A jailbird snatched the smuggled paper and looked at the sporting page.

CHAPTER XVI
BRIGANDS OF DISASTER

They brought tiger spangler from the peni-tentiary to testify in the trial of Nitro Dugan.

He could not be made to implicate Dugan in the murder for which he was serving life.

The prosecuting attorney badgered and cajoled.

Mr. Spangler did not know Mr. Dugan. He had never met him until his unfortunate arrest.

He even turned to the choleric judge with: "I'm serving life, Your Honor, for a crime committed when I was a thousand miles away." The judge rapped for order.

Prison inmates read the trial news with laughter.

Spangler was the equal of Dugan in everything but cunning.

He looked incongruous in the weird setting of the jail. Like a battleship with oars, or a lion in a trained monkey's woolen jacket. He was a massive and broad piece of muscle over six feet three. His shoulders had torn the armpits of his convict coat. There were dents in his apelike jaws, as if the chisel which shaped them had missed. His hands were enormous. His fingers were twisted; his knuckles cracked and overdeveloped.

He was under thirty, tigerish, supple, with nonchalant ruthless eyes. His mouth was hard, his lips thin, his teeth even.

So light and quick was his step that he seemed to bounce when he walked. Not even the wretched prison clothes could disguise the catlike rhythm of his body.

Always at the edges of his mouth there were wrinkles of contempt.

His hair was deep yellow. He had early been called Goldy. As his name spread over the nether world its citizens, never without a talent for apt phraseology, called him Tiger.

Always in American vagabondia, among its stronger citizens who live by bullets at night, there has persisted in growing the strong flower of loyalty.

They survive and perish by strength alone.

They ask no quarter, give none.

Into their souls is early inculcated the iron code that no man dare betray another in his own fierce calling. Murder, to them, of a helpless citizen is quite pardonable, rather regrettable. It might mean

the gallows for one who really did not mean to kill.
They kill quickly for vengeance.

They will straggle, bleeding and dying, under a
rain and clatter of bullets. But so long as a comrade
is in a pinch they remain on the battleground. If
captured they become silent as death. They shift no
blame, admit nothing.

Yeggs have swung from gallows for crimes they
did not commit rather than "peach" on a comrade
whom they knew was guilty.

"Tighten up" is the slogan. It is lived up to with
a tenacity worthy of greater men in greater causes
than masquerading with revolvers at night for the
pitiful hoardings of men more tame.

The marshal had been a reformed yegg. Two banks
in the town had been robbed twice in as many years.

It was known in yegg circles that the marshal was
an accomplice in the robberies. He had double-
crossed his fellow prowlers of the night.

In many a jungle it was told how the marshal
"got his'n."

It was a yeggs' night for a murder.

The village marshal was found at the entrance to
an alley. The strap of his club was about his wrist.
The club was gone. His revolver was also missing.
He lay on his back. His shirt and coat had been
opened. He had been shot through the heart. The
coat and shirt had been carefully buttoned again.

After receiving his share of the money from the second robbery he had shot a yegg in the back as he strolled away. The yegg died instantly.

His comrades lingered until daylight in search of the marshal. They then disappeared and waited for vengeance.

The marshal's plans were only partly correct. The dead burglar, of course, would be direct evidence to the taxpayers that the marshal had done his duty. His fatal mistake was in not considering the subterranean world from which he had emerged.

Rain lashed the buildings and ran in swift rivulets down the streets of the little town. The roar of wind and rain would drown the noise of bullets.

He stood nonchalantly under the eaves of the depot roof when a young lady alighted from the midnight train.

"Officer—could you tell me the way to the Wallsy Hotel?"

There was no vehicle in sight.

The officer volunteered to take her.

It was the last mistake of his career.

The lady held her silk umbrella low, apparently to keep the rain from beating into their faces as they passed an alley.

A man murdered on a stormy midnight would allow the perpetrators many hours for a get-away.

It was all over in a few moments.

He had been engaged on the theory that it takes a thief to catch a thief. While this rule might aptly apply to lawyers, who are fond of the phrase, it is more true in the underworld that it takes a thief to murder a thief. A thousand other thieves may know who committed the crime. If the dead gentleman has been what is known as a "rat" or a "stool pigeon" or a "doublecrosser" his grave is quickly covered by the weeds of silence.

Pity for the marshal was never expressed. Men in the underworld can never be made to understand how one can be a policeman. The latter often does turn robber. The true yegg or thief never goes over to the law unless he has first been that most hated being among mankind, a stool pigeon. The marshal had not only turned policeman, he had betrayed his kind.

"He musta been crazy—how'd he ever expect to get away with a double-cross on men like them?" was often said in the jungle. Such words were spoken among cronies. Never with "outsiders."

Much is written and said about detectives going on the road in disguise to capture brigands.

They only fool the fools.

Yeggs are betrayed but seldom, and then only from the inside. So acute do their senses become in such matters that an "outsider" can be detected at a glance.

In a gun battle with the police the yeggs are always quicker witted and more daring. Handicapped by strange locales, the fatalities are always heavier on the side of the law.

Nitro Dugan and Tiger Spangler left each morning for the courtroom, handcuffed to a guard who was slow moving and stolid. The prisoners would walk swiftly on each side of him. The guard would pull back on the handcuffs in the manner of one who held the reins on high-blooded colts.

The guard came into the jail, rattling the handcuffs.

"Come on here, burglars, an' look at the judge!"

Spangler and Dugan were handcuffed quickly.

They walked toward the steel door. The brigands were grim. The guard smiled.

Dugan's left wrist was handcuffed to the guard's right. Spangler was on the opposite side.

An officer opened the door.

The elevator waited. The Negro attendant stood outside the cage until the guard and his charges were inside.

It was three flights to go to the courtroom.

The elevator door closed.

Four men stood inside.

The Negro crashed to the floor, stiff from a rabbit blow in back of the neck.

Dugan stopped the elevator between floors. Spangler held a revolver against the guard's temple. He unlocked the handcuffs. They were placed on the guard's wrists.

Spangler threw a vicious right smash at the guard. It sent the entire lower portion of his jaw out of place. Before he sank the butt of the revolver crashed against his head.

Dugan ran the elevator swiftly to the basement.

They stepped out, closed the doors, and disappeared.

It was never learned where Spangler obtained the revolver.

CHAPTER XVII
TWENTY DOLLARS

GROWN WEARY OF BEING IN JAIL, EDDIE EVANS HAD
decided to accept the kind banker's offer. He had
gone a few days before.

"Go to the General Delivery window," he said in
parting, "I'll mail you twenty dollars."

Our sentence was drawing to a close.

He had bribed the guards to bring the things he
needed. He wore a silk scarf and a new silk shirt. A
varicolored silk kerchief hung from the breast pocket
of his coat. He left a half-filled bottle of perfume of
a rare and delicate odor.

The Old Fairy took possession of the bottle. It
was later taken from him. Its contents were sprinkled
about the washroom.

At last Eddie stood across the dead line, four feet from the door, over which prisoners dared not step.

The guard who had placed him in the hole stood near him. He smiled kindly. He had been given five dollars by the effeminate youngster.

A beautiful bark on the waves of sin, Eddie Evans literally floated out of the prison, never to be seen again.

We stood in a half circle, watching the door. It had become an obsession with me. For nearly four months I had watched men pass through it, with hands locked and heads bowed, to the most dismal of destinies.

The Negro to fifteen years, the pyromaniac to twenty, Bralen and Joe Elvin to the end of a rope, the boy from the South to brutality worse than death, the young forger to the arms of his unloved teacher.

We represented all the twisted types of life—the insane and the imbecile, the madman and the fool, the diseased and the subnormal, the senile, the vagrant, the epileptic, and the felon. We ranged from the stupidity of the Old Fairy to the intelligence of Brother Jonathon, from the timidity of Willie Richmon to the force of Tiger Spangler and Nitro Dugan.

None of us were alike. We were all treated the same.

I thought not of this at the time.

Brother Jonathon was to leave within a week after us. He paced up and down the jail the morning of our departure.

He had the manner of a patriarchal father sending his favorite sons out into a cruel world.

He admonished us grandiloquently as other jailbirds gathered about. "Always remember, my boys, that the meticulously quiet and more ornate hog must in the very nature of universal things obtain the choicest and most digestible part of the swill." He placed his hands upon us. "It is a rule made by the Divine Carpenter in Jerusalem—do good to them from whom you will obtain more good. Shoot neither a policeman nor a guard nor even a lawyer without careful aim. The Bible teaches us to be kind to animals. All needless cruelty is uncalled for in a world not made for the gentle.

"We each and all, my boys, have several things in common, hatred of our abysmally ignorant guards, and contempt for the opossums known as lawyers.

"I have not met all the lawyers in America—only a few million of them. A pickpocket is a Plato compared to them. And every crook among them has a picture of Lincoln on his wall.

"I am sorry to see you boys go out into the world. It will only cause you the embarrassment of being arrested all over again. Then, if you become a big crook, you will have to talk to lawyers.

"Some day, my lads, I am going to become the Ruler of the Universe. I will immediately place all the lawyers, guards, and wardens in status quo—or a damned strong jail.

"But trained in trickery, the lawyers would be out in an hour. And thus—my own effort at reform, like all the others, would come to nothing.

"A sad world, my boys, a sad world—in fact—a hell of a world."

The door opened at last for us.

Before stepping across the dead line with the guard I shook the old man's hand and hurried away with Blink.

Penniless, we went to the post office at once.

Eddie Evans had kept his word.

We divided the twenty dollars.

CHAPTER XVIII
BRIGHT EYES

I PARTED COMPANY WITH BLINK AND DID NOT SEE HIM again for many months.

We might have been two youths separating on our way home from school, so casual was our leave-taking.

"I think I'll beat it East," Blink said, pocketing the money.

"Well—I may run into you there," I returned.

We walked in different directions.

We were known as "road kids" in the parlance of hoboes. I first met Blink in Chicago. Nearly a hundred of us had assembled from every state in the nation. Embryo pickpockets, bruisers, and yeggs; pimps, sneak thieves and footpads; we lived, like care-free scavengers, on the very fringes of society. Out of orphanages, reform schools, and jails we had come, the sniveling and the stubborn, the mongrel and the thoroughbred, the weak and the never defeated. The youngest of us was about twelve; the oldest about fifteen. A future champion pugilist was among us, and five lads who were to serve life for murder, and fourteen others who were to be detained in different penitentiaries for lesser periods of time. One became a vaudeville headliner; another a political boss. Some were to die fighting for a nation that, with boundless generosity, had given them but hallways and box cars to sleep in. One became a Methodist minister, later falling from grace long enough to serve a term for forgery. He was then to climb back on the chariot of God, where he remained until he died insane. We were a variegated crew.

We lived at the Newsboys' Home—a faded, red-brick building that overlooked Lake Michigan. The most popular lad in the institution was this little Italian whose real name we never knew. Young as we were, many of us had something to hide, and he was reticent. We did not question him. His eyes were large, brown, and sparkling. We called him Bright Eyes.

Bright Eyes and I had reached the Home on the same winter day. Blue with the cold and very lonely, we became friends immediately. Our natures were different . . . It was the rebel in knee breeches, with tangled red hair and heavy jowl who told life to go to hell. Bright Eyes was as calm as a June morning after the rains are done.

In those hungry, wind-whipped days I hated routine as much as I do now, and every person I met tried to mold me to fit some form. But always my head stuck out. Bright Eyes was a gentleman and rebelled against life but once. A year younger than I, he was very much wiser. He knew by instinct that which I have been many years in the learning: that it doesn't pay to fight life—that, after all, it doesn't matter. One either comes through or one doesn't, and often the thoroughbred is hamstrung in the race. Life is greater than its philosophers. Bright Eyes knew that.

I remember one evening in the Home when we assembled to meet a very wealthy lady. We all read compositions that we had written. I read my own aloud, and it was greeted with applause. I had written about General Wolfe, who was my favorite hero in those days. The gray-haired and bespectacled old lady shook my hand, then turned to the matron and said, "There's literary talent displayed here." She asked my name.

It was my first literary triumph. All of us speculated as to the outcome of her remark. I lived in the clouds for three days, waiting for her limousine to come after me.

Bright Eyes said no word while I lived through

that feverish dream. Reticent as usual, he finally called me aside and said: "You'll never hear from her, Jim. Don't kid yourself. Those people can't be bothered with the likes of you and me. Look at last Christmas. Not a soul came near this joint all day."

He was right. I never heard from her again.

It was bitterly cold the week following. The wind howled from the lake for seven days and seven nights. As the Home was closed from early in the morning until late in the afternoon, Bright Eyes and I were at the mercy of the cold. We were thinly clad. We had no change of outer clothing—and no under clothing at all.

At last Bright Eyes got a job in a print shop. He had learned something of the trade somewhere. Cold as it was, I preferred the open streets, where I sold newspapers and carried luggage for travelers going from one station to another. Several bitter weeks passed.

One evening Bright Eyes returned wearing a bandage over his left eye. Some printer's ink had infected it. The eye grew worse. A doctor was called in. Three weeks later the eye was removed. . . . Unskilled in words of sympathy, we knew not what to say. For several days a sadness hung over the Home. A patch was devised to hide the empty red socket . . . the sadness passed . . . and save for depressing moments Bright Eyes was seemingly happy once again.

But we called him Bright Eyes no longer. With the terseness of our world we named him Blink.

He never returned to the print shop. He had lost interest in work. The months drifted by until spring. We took to the road, and our ways diverged.

Nearly all of us became hoboes, and so I would come across him now and then on the road, and in the underworld of some city. He always worried for fear the loss of his eye would affect the sight of the other. It became a mania with him. Cheerful liar that I was, I told him that such a thing was impossible. I argued that one-eyed people could always see better than people with two eye. Blink tried to believe me. He became a hopeless vagrant.

After years of wandering some of us settled in southern California, and there I met him again. He was still worrying about blindness, and I did my usual lying. I told him about a fellow in the navy with one eye who could see further than any other man who sailed in ships. Blink listened quietly and then said:

"God, Jim, I don't want to lose my other glim. There's so much to see!"

I immediately cut in: "But hell, Blink, you like music, and you can always hear that. And you can hear engines whistlin' far off. Bein' blind ain't so damn' bad."

"Don't kid me, Jim, I'm on. I'd rather be in jail for life—than blind. There ain't nothin' worse."

A Spanish girl passed in a riot of color, her lithe body alive with joy. Some red-winged blackbirds danced on the green grass of the plaza where we talked. Far away, through a rift in the Mexican tenements, we could see the mountains.

The Spanish girl returned, singing.

"That's a song about a bird with a broken wing," said Blink. "I wonder if he had just one glim, too."

I believe that now and then there blossoms in the world a flower that has been a thousand years in the forming. Blink had certain qualities that could be explained in no other way. His knowledge of music was astonishing. One-eyed vagabond that he was, he knew the folk music of all the nations, and he knew grand opera, too. He would go hungry to hear music; often, indeed, he would beg his way to the topmost gallery to feed his soul.

The Spanish girl's song died away. We remained tense and silent with wonder. Two heavy-footed men approached. We knew them immediately as city detectives.

"We want you as a vag," one of them said to Blink. "You've been hangin' around here long enough."

They took him to the nearest street corner and called the patrol wagon. Before I left him I said:

"Remember, Blink, you're not guilty—and stand trial."

"All right, Red," he answered with absolute unconcern.

I hurried away with the hope of helping him. We were not without friends in Los Angeles—though all of them had to be careful to avoid the trap of the law themselves. So when Blink faced the police judge the next morning five of us were there to help him. He pleaded not guilty and stood trial.

Two of our friends who went in and out of the courtroom were opium smugglers. They had hurried from the Mexican border to help a friend. When the trial was over they hurried to their work again. It was a two-hour battle. The two detectives testified, but Blink's friends proved to their own satisfaction, and evidently the judge's, that he had worked within the past six months. The young prosecutor harangued. The judge looked bored and kept gazing at a crookedly hung picture of Abraham Lincoln all through the trial. When the testimony was in he gave Blink six months in jail and suspended the sentence providing Blink got a job within a week.

In three days Blink had work as a printer's devil on a Los Angeles paper. He worked for two months at this job. But his fear of losing his other eye returned. Long weakened, it began to cause him trouble. His little band of uninfluential friends became alarmed. They persuaded him to go to the county hospital, where he lay upon a bed for four months and underwent as many operations. When the doctors had finished there were two empty red sockets in his head. The thing to do was to keep him cheerful. Yet every subject I raised seemed to be an ocular one. He would lie on the bed, his raven-black hair rolling back from his forehead, and the tears welling out of the red holes in his head like water from a spring.

He was taught the Braille system of reading, but there was no way they could bring to him the sight of sun and rain and wild, free places. So a beaten creature he became, until it was decided to send him to the Institution for the Blind. An incoherent letter came to me, and I hurried to the hospital.

"Can't you do something, Jim? I'd rather be dead than in a jail for the blind. I don't want to be caged up any more."

Between us it was decided to write to the owner of a great newspaper. Our request would be small. Surely he would use his influence to help Blink. All he wanted was the use of a street corner downtown, where he could sell newspapers.

I worked late into the night on a letter which I felt certain would touch the old general's heart. The next morning I had it typed, signed it "Frank Thomas," the name Blink used, and sent it by special delivery.

Weeks passed, but no answer came. We sent another and even more urgent letter, but it, too, remained unanswered. Another, registered, followed. It was also ignored.

Then I decided to gain an audience with the publisher by hook or crook and then switch the conversation to Blink's plight. But that was no easy matter.

After some days of consideration it dawned upon me that his wife had written many sentimental verses for his paper. I had also written sentimental verses, so it occurred to me to send samples of them, telling the publisher that Blink had written them with an ambitious letter begging an interview with the great man, telling him of my youth and the hard years, and also mentioning Ohio, for I had learned from *Who's Who in America* that he was born in my native state.

I must have written the one masterpiece of my life, for in two days I was invited to call at his home. A flunky looked at my letter to assure himself, perhaps, that I was not a labor agitator bent on murder. After some deliberation he seated me in an alcove in the hallway.

A weak-looking man sat near me. He also waited for the editor, who could.be heard in his library talking to two women who were begging money for the Y. W. C. A. The talk drifted to the last Sunday edition of his paper, and I heard the publisher ask one of the ladies if she had read his article on Henry E. Huntington, a local gentleman of wealth. The lady untactfully admitted that she had not read it. There was a pause. The lady made matters worse by trying to explain why she had not read the Sunday paper —and this was Wednesday. The editor excused himself and went upstairs. I saw him pass, scowling.

A few moments later he sent down a hundred dollars by his secretary. I could hear one of the ladies say: "Dear, dear! He gave two hundred the last time." The secretary explained that he felt that the one hundred was all he could now afford. The ladies then took their depтarture. The fact that one of them had failed to read the paper that fatal Sunday had cost the Y. W. C. A. one hundred dollars.

The secretary now invited me into the library to wait. I looked about and saw many volumes of sentimental verse by such poets as Alice and Phœbe Cary, Henry Wadsworth Longfellow, Felicia Hemans, Ella Wheeler Wilcox, Mary Howitt, and others of even lesser fame. Presently the publisher entered, followed by the weak-looking man who had waited with me in the hall. The great man turned upon him and said brusquely:

"Well, what do you want?"

The little lamb of a man faced the tiger and said:

"Well, sir, we are organizing an indemnity fund to protect such patriotic institutions as your paper against the ravages of labor agitators and socialists."

The publisher scowled and said as he paced the room restlessly:

"To hell with that damned graft! They didn't give a damn for me when my building was blown to pieces and twenty-one of my men were killed. I fought a battle, I did, for liberty and the Constitution! Without me labor would crucify all enterprise in this state."

The lamb bleated:

"But, sir, Earl Rogers thinks well of our plan!"

Earl Rogers was the brilliant lawyer who had helped Clarence Darrow defend the McNamara brothers, dynamiters, in 1911.)

It was a fatal bleat. The general threw his hands in the air and roared:

"He's a God damned—— ——"

Then, pacing up and down the floor, he delivered a long harangue on the crimes of working men. The small man would rise to go, and the general would always shout: "Sit down! Sit down!" When the gentleman managed to leave at last the busy editor turned to me and said:

"My God! Those fellows are hard to get rid of!"

I immediately committed a great social blunder. I called him Mister. He turned upon me quickly:

"General, if you please! Not that I'm vain—but young men should be taught discipline."

My hand clenched. But I thought of Blink, and was humble once again, and generaled the general all over the room. I mentioned my verses, but he preferred to rave against union labor. He stood before me, an immense man, with stooping shoulders, and heavy pouches under his eyes. His frame, once a great deal over six feet, had shriveled. He was a withered giant with a bag of skin on his bones. His eyes were close together, and all the face wrinkles converged to the corners of them. There was fanatical zeal and finality in his every utterance. Unluckily for me, the departing sheep who wanted to help the tiger fight labor—for a price—had only succeeded in putting him in an evil mood. He raved on and on. Parrying for an opening, I shot in:

"I was reading the other day, General, some verses by your distinguished wife, General, and knowing how you must have helped her, General, I have made bold to write and ask you, General, if I might not presume upon your patience, General, not for myself, General, but for a blind boy friend of mine, General, who also writes verses, General."

"Huh!" he grunted. "But would you know a piece of news if you saw it coming down the street?"

The Irish in me was still unsubdued by so mighty a presence. I replied:

"I think so, General . . . but I'm not asking for myself, General. You see, General, I have a young friend who's blind, General. He writes verses, General, and he used to work on a paper helping printers, General. One eye was fairly good when he started there, General. We ain't blamin' nobody, General. He might have lost it, anyhow, General. Though Blink claims all the towels was full of ink around the place, General."

That was unfortunate—but I was busy generaling him, and untrained in diplomacy.

"Damn it to hell, what was wrong with the towels? Everything's one damned complaint after another, by God! What in hell do you want?"

"Well, you see, General," I shot in quickly, "Blink's blind as a bat, General, and he only wants a street corner, General."

"Only wants! Oh, hell! Only wants—they all want something!"

"But this won't cost a dime, General. The judge told Blink if he didn't work he'd send him to jail, General, and Blink wants a corner downtown where he can peddle papers, General. Why, he'll sell two copies of your paper to one of any other. He's a white boy, and I've never known him to double-cross anybody."

"How long did he work for me?"

"Not long, General. His eye went gooey quick. Then it was curtains for Blink, General."

The publisher walked rapidly up and down the floor, with withered red hands behind his back, shaggy head bent low, and low wrinkles stretching across his forehead.

"I can't do anything. There's places for blind men in this state. That's why we have government and pay taxes."

"But you see," I answered, stepping before him, no longer the humble, reformed road kid, "you see, Blink's worse than blind. He has a head on him. I've seen him go nuts over a sunset. . . ." Seeing a scowl, my method changed for Blink's sake. "And he used to like your wife's poems, General, and he read your paper and believed in all you said, General. That's why he went to work for you, General. He could have started for some other paper, but he preferred to work for yours, General!"

Ignoring my scramble of words he blurted out:

"We have a State Liability Act—let that take care of him. Too many blind men peddling papers on the streets now."

"But something muffed with the State Act, General. They want to railroad him to the Blind Asylum, General. And he'll croak himself before he goes, I'm sure, General. By God! I would! I wouldn't eat their damned bread, General, if it was smeared with honey

—and Blink's been in other asylums for the poor. And so have I, General—you know what they're like."

The defiant old man, long used to the center of the stage, was ruffled by my effrontery.

"No, and I don't give a God damn," he answered.

"But, General, you have a great soul—you just gave the Y. W. C. A. some money—Blink doesn't ask for a thin dime."

"It makes no difference. The state should take care of him. He'd be in the world's way outside. There he'd be treated well."

"Maybe you're right, General—but I can't sell Blink the idea. I'd be a hypocrite if I tried."

"Well, that's enough. There's nothing I can do."

"Thank you, General," I said, and left the room.

I strolled into Westlake Park unmindful of decorated nature everywhere. I would have to lie to Blink—would have to tell him that the General would take his case under advisement. I'd have to say: "You know, kid, whenever those big guys do that something always happens. You'll have to be patient, though, Blink—those guys have a lot on their minds—and you may even have to take a ride to the blind joint for a while, and then some of us can sign a bond and get you out. This guy sure'll help us. He ain't nearly the mean guy everybody makes him out. Jack London and Clarence Darrow and that gang only have their side of it, Blink. You gotta remember that he has his side, too. Look what a lot of them guys did to his building . . ." and, so thinking, I arrived at the County Hospital.

Blink, as usual, was stretched out on his bed. His spirits were so low that he seldom had ambition enough to grope his way about the ward. To cheer him his underworld visitors would disguise their voices and make him guess who had come to see him.

I said no word that day as I stood near his bed. He touched the muscles of my forearm—his way of recognizing me—and said with a touch of gayety in his voice:

"That you, Jim? God! I'm glad."

"Yep, it's me, Blink, and I sure got some good news for you. Of course, it won't happen right away —but the general said he'd do what he could. It'll take time, though, Blink, as you know those guys are busy . . . so you'll have to be patient."

"Oh, I'll be patient, Jim. God, I'll be patient! I can't do nothin' else."

He lay back on the bed, the black tangled hair sinking into the pillow. His hand clutched mine in a feverish grasp as I looked down in his handsome face and saw, as usual, the tears gush from the holes in his head. Overcome, I leaned on his breast and sobbed, "Blink, I wish to Christ I could give you eyes . . . You could have one of mine if I could fix it so's you could!"

The hands patted my shoulders. "That's all right, Jim . . . maybe something'll happen."

"Sure thing, Blink, nobody knows. Maybe in a year some guy'll invent eyes you can see out of— they do funnier things than that."

Hope came into Blink's voice.

"I've been thinkin' about that, Jim. You know, maybe they can do that."

"Sure," I answered, "and I'll bet they'll be doin' it, too. I'll bet you they'll be takin' dead men's eyes, and fixing them in and tying up the nerves . . . so's it'll be like it was before people go blind. I was reading something about that the other day," I lied.

Three months had passed since the interview with the publisher. Christmas came. The time was drawing near for Blink's journey to the Hospital for the Blind. All his poverty-stricken friends insisted that he go to the Institution until more suitable arrangements could be made.

During Christmas week we took up a collection of nearly seventy dollars. We took the money to him with much forced banter and the words, "We're loaning you this, Blink, till you get a good corner downtown."

Always eager for news, he inquired what word had come from the publisher. I told him that I had heard from the great man's secretary the day before, and that he was taking the matter up with the City Council. This news appeased him somewhat, and we talked of old times until it was time for me to go.

The hospital, situated as it was on a busy thoroughfare, was no easy place for a blind man to escape from. Yet Blink did escape—after the lights had been put out, the night before he was to be sent to the asylum. The city of Los Angeles was four miles away, and the path taken there by a blind man must have been a devious one.

But Blink found his way to a cheap hotel, where the landlady gave him a room with another blind man. In the center of this room was an oilcloth-covered table. She asked Blink to be as tidy as possible and place everything on it. She let her little boy lead him about the next afternoon.

He asked the lad to go to a motion picture theater with him—"where there was music." It was a continuous show and they remained for hours. The youngster became restless, so Blink paid him a dollar to remain another hour. Then he asked to be led to a pawnshop.

When I found that Blink had escaped I inquired in his old haunts. No one knew where he had gone. I spent the afternoon looking for him, without success, but felt reassured because of the money he had.

That evening a package addressed to Joe Bertucci and me came by special messenger. It was wrapped about with many rubber bands. They ran in every direction. The address was written with lead pencil and was hardly legible.

The package of brown paper contained fifty-one dollars in paper, gold, and silver, of different denominations. The bills were crunched, the silver and gold loose among the paper. The letter read:

"I thought I'd send this back to you guys so the dicks won't get it when they search the room. I won't need it any more. Please forgive me, fellows, it was the only way out."

The letter was badly scrawled. Some of the lines overlapped.

I hurried to the address the messenger had given me. Blink, gentleman to the end, had placed his head on the oilcloth-covered table before he drilled a hole through it with the revolver the pawnbroker had sold him.

The next morning the *Times* carried a little story to the effect that Frank Thomas, a printer, had committed suicide in a cheap hotel.

There was no funeral for Blink and no headstone. I did not believe in such things. A young Irish burglar wanted to pray for him every night. I told him to go ahead. He was later sentenced for life as a habitual criminal. I hope it has not interfered with his praying for Blink's soul. For I believe he had one.

When it was all over, Joe Bertucci watched, with

me, a conglomerate throng pass the haunts Bright
Eyes had loved.

"Well I guess the kid was right, Jim," he said.
"It was the best way out."

I made no answer.

CHAPTER XIX
A CALIFORNIA HOLIDAY

I_T_ HAPPENED MANY YEARS LATER. A MAN WAS ABOUT
to be legally murdered in a California penitentiary.

I was sent to describe the event for H. L. Mencken.

I visited the prison known as San Quentin a few
days before. My errand at that time was one of friend-
ship for several inmates.

San Quentin stretches drab and sun scorched along
the blue waters of San Francisco Bay. Majestic clouds
seem always to be riding the heavens on the watery
horizon. Boats glide, far out on the bay, as if fearful
of drawing too near the crowded castle of the doomed.

Originally built for less than two thousand prisoners, it now houses thirty-six hundred, about one hundred of whom are women. The roads are graveled.
There is a detour sign two miles from the prison upon
which is printed in large black letters beneath a
hand pointing prisonward:

THIS IS THE RIGHT ROAD

The front of the prison is grass and flower bedecked. A horseshoe, token of good luck, is over the main gate. In spite of its beautiful setting it is, to me, the dreariest of American prisons—a place where the music of the spheres is ragtime.

About twenty miles from San Francisco, the most charming of American cities, San Quentin is often bathed in fogs and lacerated with cold winds. The very sea gulls seem to fly over it with the monotony of despair. The guards live and bring up their children in the fear of God and the law within a few hundred yards of where men are hanged with sanctimonious gesture.

I had called to visit several prisoners. A reporter for the San Francisco *Examiner* accompanied me. The city editor had telephoned the warden of our arrival. Less than a month on the job, the new warden, a man hunter all his life, was unusual in that he had none of the illiterate man's blind acceptance of life.

A very quiet man, between fifty and sixty, slightly stooped, with most of his upper teeth missing, he might have been the leader of a Salvation Army band, instead of one who had long been known to be quick on the trigger. A Hindu had once run amuck in a crowded courtroom. The new warden had drilled him dead with a bullet. That was his claim to fame in California.

He took us to the office of the captain of the guard. We walked through three iron gates before reaching the interior yard. Save for the small walks, this yard was literally covered with blooming flowers of many sizes and colors. After the drab cement and iron bars, and the stern dull faces of the guards, the contrast was startling.

We waited in this room until my friends arrived. They were Kid McCoy, Robert Joyce Tasker, Joe Mackin, and Paul Kelly.

Mackin, a shriveled little ex-jockey, perhaps with the seeds of a writer about to germinate in his head, doing a fifteen year jolt for highway robbery. Tasker, twenty-four, tall, good looking, a sheik type for society girls and stenographers, with black hair carefully combed, doing five to twenty-five years for holding up a crowded dance hall. He is now the associate editor of the San Quentin *Bulletin* and a contributor to the *American Mercury*.

As gruff old Carlyle might have said: "By such incontrovertible ways do men find themselves."

Kelly, accidentally caught up with bootleg gin and a woman, spasmodically married, was now working a loom in the jute mill, that modern California inferno which drives even dull men mad.

It is a place where a yell subsides to a whisper, so great is the whirring noise. Particles of hemp dust fly all about the mill. Wheels, pulleys, and machines roar with deafening noise. A convict must do his task each day—so many sacks, so much twine, or be penalized if he fails.

I had known Kelly in happier days. Generous, a square dealer, with the pride and the laughter of the Gael, life had always been to him a Lambs Club frolic.

And now the crows of trouble were walking around his eyes. The smile on his face was hard pushed to keep back the tears. An actor, Thomas Meighan, had contributed ten thousand dollars for his defense. Other friends had rallied to him.

Sensational newspapers, a corporation lawyer untrained in mob psychology, a shallow judge, and middle-class hatred of Hollywood had done for Kelly.

It was no time now for the imbecilities by which more fortunate men try to placate others in trouble.

The conversation lagged. There was a pause. Kelly's body trembled in its ill-fitting gray and hemp-dusty suit.

"Well, Paul—all you can do is take your jolt," I finally said.

"But I didn't kill him—I didn't kill him," and then, "God!—but it's great to get away from that jute mill—you've got to live it, Jim—to know it— there's no other way."

"I know, Paul—you're right—I'd rather read one

page by a man who had been in hell—than all of Dante."

I watched his face. The deep lines running down from the eyes were those of an emotional man forced by the exigencies of circumstance and environment into a withering restraint. We walked toward Kid McCoy and the warden. The once great pugilist was saying, "I'll tell you, Warden—Tunney hasn't got a chance—no man has with Dempsey when he's right. There's too many big words in Tunney's head."

Not wishing to rob McCoy of a moment's pleasure, I turned my head.

Through the flowers, followed by a guard, walked a young girl, slim and beautiful. In white blouse and dark skirt, her hair carefully combed, and with blue laughing eyes, she seemed a pretty high school girl on her way to an easy lesson.

"Who's that?" I asked Paul Kelly.

"It's the jazz murderess," he replied. "The kid who killed her mother." It was as if McCoy had smashed me under the heart. Another prisoner, perhaps seeing my expression, said, "There's all kinds in here, Jim."

Tasker and the reporter joined us. Soon we bade the four men good-bye and walked into the garden.

The warden went to his lunch. We walked toward the hospital. The reporter wished to ask the prison physician, Dr. L. L. Stanley, a question. There was a rumor that certain other prisoners had lately tried to kill the Rev. Herbert Wilson, arch bandit, murderer, informer, and one-time Baptist minister, with a poisoned arrow.

We accompanied Dr. Stanley to the dining room. The man who waited upon our table was Tom Mooney, whose conviction as a dynamiter stirred the nations of the world. Still in middle life, the years are nevertheless crawling heavily across Mooney. Though even the intercession of Woodrow Wilson failed to get him a new trial, he still hopes for a pardon. A naïve man, he dreams of justice.

Allowed to languish in prison the past dozen years, he is neglected by the parlor radicals, now grazing in more luscious publicity fields. Men high in financial power have said of Mooney: "Well, if he's not guilty of the Preparedness Day bombing, he's guilty of something else. He belongs in San Quentin." Mooney's enemies are unlike his friends; they know exactly what they want.

Mooney, now phonographic, talked for an hour, detailing his acquittals and convictions. If he is innocent, it seems incomprehensible that semicivilized men should be guilty of such a crime. But even Sinclair Lewis suppressed the hardness of a Babbitt to gain his end.

"Well, Tom," said the reporter, "if they let you out to-morrow, what would you do?"

Mooney stood erect, the picture of subdued virility. "I'll tell you what I'd do—I'd look after my health right away."

All of us glanced at the physician. No man spoke for a minute.

"What's the matter with your health, Tom?" the doctor finally asked.

"No reflections on you, Doctor," returned Mooney, "but you know how it is," and then further explanations, which wended back to the injustice of twelve years' imprisonment.

Those years have eaten at the mind of Mooney, stooping his shoulders. They have carved hollow places beneath his eyes.

As he went to the kitchen the doctor said, "It's the first time I've ever heard his story—you know there's thirty-six hundred of them here."

The reporter asked if the newspaper report of Clara Phillips' attempted suicide were true. "No, it wasn't," he replied, "but it's a wonder all the women don't go mad—cooped up the way they are." The corners of his mouth twitched with pity.

Dr. Stanley listens to the last heartbeats of gallows-hung men. He remains kindly, even sentimental over the most atrocious of his charges.

He talked of Bluebeard Watson, said to be a hermaphrodite, convicted of having married and killed many women.

"It will be centuries before anyone is able to give Watson's case justice. He's my head nurse over in the hospital. He makes pets out of birds. There's nothing he won't do for a sick man. He nurses them as tenderly as a woman. I wish you'd say something about him. He's in here forever—he'll never get out—so all you can get him is a little understanding."

Eager to change the subject, I said, "You've been here a great many years, haven't you, Doctor?"

"Yes, yes," he half drawled, "a good many years. I went into private practice a short time, but I gave it up and came back. Got homesick, I guess."

Someone told the story of a ball-throwing contest in which a condemned young dope fiend had participated. He was soon to dangle in a noose.

Three thousand prisoners cheered the lad who was soon to leave for another country. Strangely enough, no contestant was in good form that day. Even the champion ball thrower, a giant Negro, was off. The youth won, amid cheers.

He died in the belief that he could throw a ball farther than any man in prison. Ego attends us all.

As we talked to the doctor there appeared James McNamara, the labor agitator, convicted of blowing up the Los Angeles *Times* Building and killing twenty-one people, and now serving his fifteenth year of a life sentence.

Steel-gray eyes, perfect features, about forty-five

years of age. McNamara smiled when asked if he were on the Los Angeles *Times* mailing list. Five years before I had said to him, "You'll get out soon."

His reply was: "What an optimist you are, Jim! Did you make four-minute speeches during the war? Tom Mooney's innocent and *he* can't get out. How long do you think they'll keep *me?*" Then with emphasis, "I'm supposed to have killed twenty-one men."

McNamara was then in charge of the condemned row. I had told him the outline of a novel in which a youthful radical was to be hanged. He was much interested in the plan.

He was eager to help me get the correct details and atmosphere. He talked of my embryonic leading character as though he were a reality.

"You want to get it right," he said, "it'll help the cause."

He had followed my career and always asked me, "Are you still going to do the story of the boy?"

And now, in leaving me, he said, "You ought to come over Friday, Jim, they'll top a guy here then. It'll be what you want for your book."

Topping is the prison term for hanging.

On Friday morning at six o'clock I started again for San Quentin with Raymond Griffith, the actor, and Malcolm Waldron, a reporter for the San Francisco *Call*. Fremont Older, that most humane of editors, had asked me to write a description of the execution.

The man was to mount the thirteen steps leading to the gallows at ten o'clock. The newspaper wanted a preliminary story. A morbid public was interested in how he had passed the night, and even what he had eaten for breakfast. Hence the early start.

As we huddled back from the foggy wind on the bay Griffith said: "They talk of Nietzsche and all that gang—why, those birds were soft! The real hard people are the Baptists, the Methodists, the Puritans. Nietzsche couldn't hang a man like this."

"Cromwell, for instance," I suggested.

"Yes—that's the guy—now, he *was* hard."

Said Waldron: "I covered a hanging in the East, and we were all given black coffee before we went to the death room. I wonder if they'll do that here?"

While Griffith tried to see Paul Kelly I went with Waldron. At the door of the warden's office was a plaster bust of Senator Hiram Johnson. Spectacles were upon it to accentuate the likeness. The artist seemed to have difficulty in adjusting the Senator's scarf. He compromised by allowing it to hang under his collar.

We met two other reporters in the office.

"Now listen, fellows," said Waldron, "we'll make a gentleman's agreement. There's only two 'phones here—so let's all 'phone our stories in together."

"All right," they agreed.

That weighty matter settled, we greeted the warden's clerk. He was frozen indifference. The clerk of the Prison Board, a two-hundred-pound porpoise of a man, with a neck bulging over his collar, entered the room.

"Meet the newspaper boys here," suggested the warden's clerk.

"I'll meet 'em later," was the terse reply.

"It's mutual," returned a reporter as the clerk of the board passed into another room. From another reporter:

"That guy hates us—God, I'm glad! You know it's funny about these hangings. I knew a fellow who covered thirty of them. He fainted at the last one."

It was not eight-thirty.

"Damn this waiting around," blurted a reporter whose eyes were swollen from a night's debauch. "The time sure drags."

"It may for us," put in Waldron, "but I'll bet it flies for *him*."

We remained silent for some time.

"That's right—the poor devil," at last came from the reporter with the swollen eyes—then, smiling, "It won't be long now."

"Is it true they give them a shot of booze or dope before they bump them?" The remark was delivered to the warden's clerk.

He answered, "This guy says, 'A glass o' whisky.' Send up a barrel of it!" The clerk left.

"Well, it won't be long now," said the blear-eyed reporter for a second time, in the midst of a news competitor's words.

"I think it was here that they used to grant a fellow's dying request before they strung him up." He smiled. "A Negro asked the warden if he couldn't dance a jig on the gallows. That was a hard one for the warden, but he finally consented. The chaplain objected strenuously, though, in the name of dignity and religion, so the poor shine had to keep his feet still."

I watched a pelican sailing beautifully toward the sun. Waldron touched my arm. "A miserable business for 1927—eh?"

"You've just got the fidgets, Waldron," I bantered as the warden entered the room.

His face sagged as if weights were on his chin. The warden of a California prison is forced to see all executions. His raised hand sends the doomed man downward. It was this warden's first.

"How do you feel?" a reporter asked.

"All right," he answered slowly, removing the pipe from his half toothless mouth. "It's not pleasant to jerk a man into the great beyond."

We agreed in silence and said no more while the warden remained in the room.

Waldron, looking toward the bay, said nervously, "Gee—the grass is nice and green—the sun's warm —even the sea gulls are more beautiful than I've ever seen them before."

We all knew his drift. Our minds were with him.

"Be a realist, Waldron," I jerked at him. "You mean it's hell to die on a morning like this."

He murmured weakly, "Yes."

"Well, it surely is hell," I half laughed, with the hope of lifting Waldron's mood, when my own was no higher. "But this fellow, Earl Clark, certainly got a tough break. If a fellow read about it in a book he wouldn't believe it. He escaped from the county jail in Los Angeles after he was convicted, and he beat it to this little town in South Dakota—married a girl who didn't know a thing about his record, and went into the painting business. He was getting along fine when a young kid who'd taken a mail-order course to become a detective turned him in. He was really making good, you know. Clark was supposed to have carried poison to bump himself off if they ever caught him, but he was too slow. I see where Frank Dewar, the jailer down in Los Angeles, wired the governor that there was even a chance that he wasn't guilty."

"He was guilty all right"—from a voice behind a desk.

"You'd think they'd give a fellow at least a life term after that," said Waldron.

"But there's six feet of grass over the other guy—remember that," threw in the warden's clerk. No man answered.

"The guy was sentimental, that's all," said the reporter with the bleared eyes. "He killed a sailor because he brought a red rose to his girl every night. Why didn't he wait a while—the sailor would have gone to sea—they all do—don't they?"—looking at me as if I knew.

"Yes—I guess so—I think that's their job."

"But who was the dame?" the reporter asked.

"Just a broad," was the reply from somewhere.

"Just a broad," two voices took up.

"A million-dollar price for a ten-cent woman," said the reporter with the swollen eyes as we walked toward the main entrance.

At least seventy men in citizens' clothes stood in groups. I could tell by their faces that many were guards and detectives.

It was now twenty minutes of ten.

We marched one by one through the flower garden. A guard, laughing outright, pointed his club at a marching gentleman, and said, "He's turnin' pale already." Several of the marchers laughed.

Prisoners looked out of the hospital windows at life marching to see death. The subserviency of iron bars could not obliterate their contempt for us from their faces.

This section of the prison had the appearance of an abandoned sawmill. The accumulated débris of generations was about us.

To the left of the hospital was the condemned row where other cattle, in prison vernacular, awaited their chance to meet the Christians' God. Down a little hill we walked, passing on our left a heavy iron door with a large padlock upon it. It was the entrance to the cooler, where all was pitch darkness—eighteen stone cages of icy torture and Zolaesque despair.

The authorities often place men there for infractions of prison rules. They are given a diet of bread and water and their own thoughts, if any, on the mercy of mankind.

Farther on was the butcher shop—the morgue. Above us was a herder with a loaded rifle. I noted that the guards did not carry guns inside the prison. The reason seemed obvious. In a wild scramble of mutiny or for freedom the convicts might disarm them.

We reached the rear of the prison and walked down a less pretentious alley. We stopped at the foot of aged stairs which projected about five feet from the wall. They reached three flights. Fearful of the rickety steps, about twenty men were allowed upon them at a time. We now went two by two. Waldron walked with me.

A fat man grumbled at the long flight of steps. "They do hangin's better in Folsom," he panted.

A guard near the railing commanded, "Step lively there!" I recognized his face. He was the Irish gentleman who had long before commented, "It used to be a good graft—sellin' the rope—a dollar an inch—now the board makes us burn it."

And then, at the foot of the gallows, in showing me a leather contraption, he elucidated, "We put 'em in here if they wriggle." My mind on the Irish boy I was to hang in a book, I remembered.

As I counted the seventy-five decrepit steps I had the diabolical wish that they would crumple beneath us. "Wouldn't it be funny," I said to Waldron, "if all of us croaked before Clark?"

He made no answer. His mouth was tight shut. His eyes betrayed the life-hurt dreamer.

The debonair Griffith walked behind me. His face was more impassive than a Chinaman's at a lottery. I stumbled as I watched it. "Careful," he said as we turned in on the third floor.

We passed through the print shop. Four prisoners sat at desks, editing the prison paper. Tacked to the walls were the pictures of actresses of a long ago period. They looked smilingly grotesque in the abominable costumes and hats which were then in style.

"Convicts, forever free, must have tacked them there," I thought. Musing on the sex agonies of men in prison, I became more tolerant of the fatuous faces which stared from the lithographs.

Inside a small room were three prisoners. Thin, with suppressed leers and furtive eyes, they lolled about in the manner of laborers before the day's work begins. They were the scavenger crew. It was their job to take the dead man from the rope, place him in a fine coffin made by other convicts, and hurry him to the little cemetery on the hill where rest the men with broken necks.

We now halted in front of a large door, opening into a room which contained the gallows.

It was ten minutes of ten.

I stood within a half-dozen feet of the coffin. A guard with a hard, flat face, not over thirty, leaned upon it. Another guard approached. "Here's his overcoat," smiled the first guard.

I touched Waldron's arm. His body trembled.

The shuffling of feet stopped. One could literally hear hearts beat. A sinuous three-quarter length picture of Lillian Russell smiled above the coffin at the nonchalant legality of murder. I started to say some words to Griffith. They rattled in my throat.

The door opened. We marched into the room of death.

It must have been sixty feet long and thirty wide. Save for the gallows, it was bare. It was painted a sickly blue, like a Kansas sky after a tornado. The death cell was about thirty feet from the gallows. It was also painted blue. It was quite large, the ceiling very high. A gas jet, about three feet long, hung from the center.

One rope, already knotted, hung from the gallows. About were three small ropes, one of which held the trap. In seven minutes they were to be cut by three guards. In this way, no man knew which one had sent the body dangling in the air. There was a small platform at the bottom. Thirteen steps led to the gallows. They were worn with the feet of many men who never came down alive.

Other lines of rope stretched from the ceiling. They were in different stages of testing process through which each rope must pass before its last service. The ropes were all new; they are used but once. To each was attached a tag bearing the name and execution date of the next man to die.

After a man is hanged his picture is placed, along with many others, behind a large glass in an adjustable frame. It stands in the Bertillon room. No face seems natural. By, perhaps, some thought transformation which takes place in each brain at the time the picture is taken, each mouth seems puckered as though the rope were quicker than the lens.

It was two minutes to ten.

The room was closed tightly. Not a rift of air entered. We were aware that a man must be pronounced dead before any of us could leave the room. Each one of us looked toward the raised gallows.

The warden and two doctors faced the gallows.

An oppressive silence rolled in waves through the room. The hinges of a door creaked. The doomed man entered. The chaplain preceded him.

His neck was bare. His eyes were wide open, glassy. His mouth sagged, as if too tired to appeal to ears that could not hear. His knees bent. All power of locomotion had gone from his legs. The eyes seemed to see nothing. His arms were strapped to his sides. Under each armpit was the hand of a heavy guard. Their iron arms did not bend. The man was literally carried to the trap. His legs were strapped together. The hood was pulled over his head. He turned slightly, as if to say a word. The rope was adjusted. The chaplain read from his book in a dreadful monotone. I recall the words: "Confide his soul to the mercy of God." The warden's hand raised. The trap sprang with an awful noise. The man's body dropped ten feet. It did not move.

A small stepladder was placed in front of the body. The sometime sentimental doctor stood upon it, ripped the dying man's shirt down to his heart, and applied a stethoscope. A convict, in the rear, held the body firm. An assistant physician held the victim's hand. Every now and then he would feel the pulse. I watched the hand become stiff and turn blue.

Griffith, the comedy actor, had turned his face to the wall. There were tears in his eyes. Waldron gulped. The warden stood, eying the slowly dying man. He might have been posing for the tragedy of mankind. He swallowed often. His hands opened and closed.

The minutes dragged, like horribly wounded soldiers, into eternity. A man held a watch near me.

A crash came at six minutes after ten. A two-hundred-pound railroad detective fainted to the floor. Men scrambled to carry him away. "It had to be a fellow that size," murmured someone. I thought it was Griffith. I smiled grimly. Suddenly, in a far corner, another form crashed to the floor. It was a very large policeman. "Another two-hundred-pounder," whispered the same voice. It was now eight minutes after ten.

The doctor listened patiently, even tenderly, with his stethoscope. The warden still watched. Vengeance seemed to have fled temporarily from the hearts of all in the room.

Life was pumped from the powerful chest slowly. It was thirteen minutes after ten before the man was pronounced dead. The rope was cut. The scavenger crew came.

I hurried with Waldron to get a statement from the warden. As if fearful of comment, he eluded the writing craft.

The other reporters had vanished.

"Gosh, I hope they don't double-cross me," was Waldron's comment, as we rushed down the rickety stairs.

A guard yelled, "Hey there, you paddocks." We stopped. "You guys wait for the rest of the gang." When the other men joined us we marched out.

Once released from the curiosity brigade, we dashed into a telephone booth in the front office of the penitentiary. Waldron telephoned his story and my impressions to the *Call*. Mistrusting our fellow writers, we scooped them by accident.

We found them in the warden's office, busily telephoning their papers. Something else had happened.

The doomed man who in bidding farewell to the warden in the death cell had said to him, "I'll see you again if I'm lucky," had also left him a letter.

The reporters scrambled over the letter. Then two men copied it as another reporter read it aloud over the telephone.

The governor had refused to commute the dead man's sentence on account of his prison record. The letter, scribbled on coarse paper with a soft lead pencil, read:

DEAR WARDEN:

Many thanks for the kind treatment. I know how you feel, sir, and, believe me, I can sympathize with you—it's your first and I hope your last. I have only a few minutes and I want to say now with my last breath that I had no more to do with De Silve's death than you did.

I don't blame the jury—how can I when the state's witness lied?—yes, two of them. The rest told the truth. But with a poor lawyer and a record the verdict would have been the same had I been charged with the death of Abe Lincoln.

Yes, I have one prison record and two $50 fines against me. The rest is just arrests—no charge, or just "vag"—not even a jail term. My prison term was for a $14 check—for which I was pardoned.

Thank you again. Good-bye, Warden,

Sincerely yours,

E. J. Clark.

On the margin was scrawled:

This is true, so help me God. Just a few minutes to go.

THE END

JIM TULLY CHRONOLOGY: LIFE AND WORKS

1886: Born June 3, near St. Marys, in Auglaize County, Ohio, the son of ditch digger James Dennis Tully and Maria Bridget "Biddy" (née Lawler) Tully

1892: Mother dies May 1 at age 35

1892–98: Spends six years at St. Joseph's Orphan Asylum in Cincinnati

1898–1900: Works through record-cold winter during a year and a half at the farm of Solomon Boroff in Van Wert County, Ohio

1901–07: Travels the country as a road kid and a hobo

1907: Leaves the road in June, settling in Kent, Ohio

1907–10: Works as a chainmaker and boxes as a lightweight

1910: Goes to work for Davey Tree in Kent (first writing published in *Davey Tree Surgeon's Bulletin*)

Marries Florence Bushnell in Kent on October 14

1911: First professional print appearance, the poem "On Keats' Grave," published June 27 in the *Cleveland Plain Dealer*

Son, Thomas Alton, born on August 3

1912: Settles with family in Los Angeles

1914: Meets early literary idol Jack London

1917: Daughter, Trilby Jeanne, born on November 13

1921: Separates from first wife, Florence, in November

1922: First book, *Emmett Lawler*, published by Harcourt, Brace

1923: Divorced from Florence on October 28

1924: Second book, *Beggars of Life*, published by A&C Boni

1924–25: Works for Charlie Chaplin

1925: Marries Margaret R. "Marna" Meyers on January 24

Completes The Life of Thomas H. Ince (never published)

Maxwell Anderson's adaptation of *Beggars of Life*, *Outside Looking In*, opens in New York with young James Cagney as Tully

1926: Hollywood novel, *Jarnegan*, published by A&C Boni

Black Boy, play written with Frank Dazey, opens in New York with Paul Robeson in the starring role

1927: *Circus Parade* published by A&C Boni

Completes *Life of Charlie Chaplin* (never published)

Twenty Below, play written with Robert Nichols, published by Robert Holden & Company (London)

1928: *Shanty Irish* published by A&C Boni

Play version of *Jarnegan*, adapted by Charles Beahan and Garrett Fort, opens on Broadway

Director William Wellman's film version of *Beggars of Life*, starring Louise Brooks, Wallace Beery, and Richard Arlen

1929: With Marna, travels to Ireland, Great Britain, and France, meeting George Bernard Shaw, H.G. Wells, and James Joyce.

1930: *Shadows of Men* published by Doubleday, Doran & Co.

Beggars Abroad published by Doubleday, Doran & Co.

Divorced from second wife, Marna, on February 26

Knocks out John Gilbert during February fight at Hollywood's Brown Derby

Featured in the MGM film *Way for a Sailor*, co-starring with John Gilbert and Wallace Beery

1931: *Blood on the Moon* published by Coward-McCann, Inc.

1932: *Laughter in Hell* published by A&C Boni

Film version of *Laughter in Hell* with Pat O'Brien

Purchases three-and-a-half acres on a peninsula point on Toluca Lake and construction begins on a stone and red-brick home he will call Tall Timbers

1933: Marries third wife, Myrtle Zwetow, on June 26

1934: Travels to Mexico City to interview artist Diego Rivera

1935: *Ladies in the Parlor* published by Greenbrrg

Writer Langston Hughes and boxer Henry Armstrong are guests for lunch at Tall Timbers

Son, Alton, pleads guilty to attacking a sixteen-year-old girl and is sentenced to San Quentin for one to fifty years

1936: *The Bruiser* published by Greenberg

Purchases a one-hundred acre ranch, Faraway Farm, near Canoga Park

1940: Sells Tall Timbers and moves to Faraway Farm

Daughter, Trilby, marries airplane mechanic Raymond Beamon

1941: Alton paroled and released from San Quentin

Suffers a heart attack a few days after Christmas

1942: *Biddy Brogan's Boy* published by Scribner's

1943: *A Dozen and One* published by Murray & Gee

1947: Dies June 22 at Cedars of Lebanon hospital

BOOKS BY JIM TULLY

Emmett Lawler (1922) (New York: Harcourt, Brace and Company, Inc.)

Beggars of Life (1924) (New York: Albert & Charles Boni)

Jarnegan (1926) (New York: Albert & Charles Boni)

Circus Parade (1927) (New York: Albert & Charles Boni)

Twenty Below (1927) with Robert Nichols, play, (London: Robert Holden & Co. Ltd.)

Shanty Irish (1928) (New York: Albert & Charles Boni)

Shadows of Men (1930) (New York: Doubleday, Doran and Company)

Beggars Abroad (1930) (New York: Doubleday, Doran and Company)

Blood on the Moon (1931) (New York: Coward-McCann, Inc.)

Laughter in Hell (1932) (New York: Albert & Charles Boni)

Ladies in the Parlor (1935) (New York: Greenberg: Publisher)

The Bruiser (1936) (New York: Greenberg: Publisher)

Biddy Brogan's Boy (1942) (New York: Charles Scribner's Sons)

A Dozen and One (1943) (Hollywood: Murray & Gee, Inc.)

Reprints of *Beggars of Life, Circus Parade, Shanty Irish,* and *The Bruiser* available from Black Squirrel Books, an imprint of Kent State University Press.

Reprints of *Shadows of Men* and *Blood on the Moon* available from Commonwealth Book Company, St. Martin, Ohio.

MAJOR ADAPTATIONS OF BOOKS BY JIM TULLY

Outside Looking In by Maxwell Anderson (play version of *Beggars of Life,* produced in New York in 1925)

Jarnegan by Charles Beahan and Garrett Fort (play version of Tully's novel, produced in New York in 1928)

Beggars of Life by Benjamin Glazer (film version of Tully's book, directed by William Wellman and released by Paramount Pictures in 1928)

Laughter in Hell (film version of Tully's novel, starring Pat O'Brien and released by Universal Pictures in 1932)